Published by DBrockman Publishing

DBrockman Publishing,
1007 E Brandon Blvd #633
Brandon, Fl 33511
dbpublisher@yahoo.com

ISBN 979-8-2181157-5-3

Publishers Note: This is a work of Fiction. The characters, incidents,
and the dialogue are drawn from the author's imagination and are
not to be constructed as real. Any resemblance to actual events or
persons (living or dead) is entirely coincidental.

n the 'MUCK'
ng in Tampa, F
s at the Univers
ed when I was i
hich could be v
ed in the Etern:
. I received a T
Poetry Poem co
g computers, n

This book is r
This book is
at an early ag
was born in :
One day whil
up in a house
with the law v
move to Tamp.
to offer. Tampa
one could ever im
passion, excitement, and its very emotional.

ng its my first
hat saw a lot ol
ng as she got ol
of Bil om, Missi
e found her mo
had a misunder
back up overnig
Big City had m
Silky out in the v
a thnlling book full o

I'm In love

w

Loving   1e !

Author dexter orockman sr.

dbrockman publishing

RAW WRITTENS

The next three stories are case files from a short series book I will be completing called the KIT Files. ENJOY!

My First Case

"So, to make sure I fully understand you... This guy has been trying to turn himself in for a home invasion he committed months ago, but there has not been any reports in that area?" I asked with a questionable look of concern.

"Yes." The detective responded firmly. "K.I.T, that's what you go by, is that correct?" He asked as if he didn't already have my files in fron of him.

"That is correct, sir." I responded as firm as his yes. He read through my files and he knows this is my first real case. This was a case the detectives didn't want to deal with so they decided to hire a P.I (Private Investigator) to do the leg work. Being I was new in the field, they could afford my prices and knew I would go above and beyond to make an impression for my first case.

"So, 'K.I.T' all we need you to do is question our potential suspec do your lil Private I ish, find out who house this guy broke into and see what grounds we have to detain him." The detective instructed as he closed the files.

"Yes sir, that I can do." I replied as I launched from my chair feeling like I was 'Chase-On-The-Case'!

"Listen kid. As strange as this..."

"The name is K.I.T, sir." I corrected him while interrupting his sentence.

"Whatever. K.I.T, as I was saying... As strange as this may seem, people try and turn themselves in more than you imagine. Some are homeless, some are mentally challenged and many other farfetched reasons. We have evaluated this guy and he seems sane and he has a jo and a place to live. So just find out what you can so we can close this case."

"You have my word and my dedication, sir."

He stood up extended his hand and said, "Thanks kid." I cringe my face and gripped his hand firmly. "Sorry, I mean K.I.T!" I smiled as I gathered my things to leave his office.

"Good morning Mr. Ian. My name is K.I.T and I am a part of the investigating team here." I have learned from mocked cases to never out right tell them you are a P.I. Suspects will feel reluctant to sharing information, also they get this notion they don't have to be lawful.

"Good morning K.I.T." He expressed as he took his seat. "How are you on this fine morning?" I could tell he was a manner able man. His body frame was not pleasant, he seemed a little out of shape, but sometimes perception could lead to deception. This guy was in his late thirties, he had a clean cut and his causation skin looked like he did outside work or went to a tanning salon.

"I am doing quite well, thanks for asking." He knotted his head as he awaited a follow-up question. I made small talk to open him up to me before questioning. "You seem like a rounded guy with a level head on your shoulder, what makes you want to turn yourself into the police, what crime did you commit?

He dropped his head and said in a low voice. "I broke into a lady house." He slowly raised his he awaiting my response.

"Well, the paper work I have in front of me told me that much, can you give me details onto why you decided to break in. Even after doing so, you never got caught, but yet you are sitting here trying to turn yourself in on a crime that has not been reported."

He leaned back in his chair and began to tell his story: "So, it all started a few a months ago. I was eating lunch at Hollywood's Cafe. These two guys came in and sat at the table behind me. I found myself ear hustling their table talk. One of the guys spoke abou..."

"Hold on, 'Ear Hustling'?" I asked interrupting him mid sentence. was like I had BNU. Brain Not Understanding.

"Yes, it's when you unwittingly listen in on a conversation and gathering mental information. It's like what writers do when they run out of material or get writers block and want a fresh idea."

"Oh, ok. Continue with your story."

"Ok, as I was saying. One of the guys were talking about a group they formed for men. The group is designed to take back the respect women don't have for men anymore."

"Oh really..." He looked over at her. "Sorry, that slipped out."

"Cool." He stated as he continued. "After the guys finished talking one guy left and I approached the guy about the organization."

"What is this Organization and did you join it?" I asked before I could think.

"The group is called E.R.A.P... Well, I sort of joined it. When I was talking to the guy he made some really valuable and valid points."

"Oh, what were they may I ask?" I'm sure he could tell I was getting defensive, but I couldn't take much of his story about his JT Money Hoe hating Posse grown men/Boy Group he'd joined.

I began to get tense. He took a deep breath as he explained. "There were a few things he said pertaining women. The one that caught my attention was how men love harder than women. Men kill themselves and other men over women. Examples are; Othello, Romeo, Samson, David killing Bashiba husband, Adam and Eve. Women are cause of their death."

"Hold up, Eve didn't kill Adam. He died of old age and natural causes." I stressed waiting to see how he would rebuttal.

"I bet you still think Eve ate a fruit from a tree huh? It was no fruit; she ate a dick and liked it. She liked it so much she went back to Adam and told him what she had done. She persuaded him. That's how they knew they were naked. She fucks the Serpent, told Adam, sucked and fucked him. Then Adam had to live with the fact that his wife fucked the baddest mother fucker on the planet. That's the natural cause that killed him."

I grew silent and in plenty thoughts. I'd never looked at it like that but this dude went from Dr. Jekyll to Mr. Hyde. A smirk came over my face. "Boy, you silly." That was all I could say.

He leaned forward and said, "Think about it, what it means when they say 'Be Fruitful', huh? Why you think Kane killed Abel? Cause Eve was still getting side dick from the Serpent. Kane was a devil child."

"You know what, I need a break. Let's take a fifteen and meet me back here."

"You thinking bout what I said huh?" I walked out as he was still trying to finish his lecture.

1226 - 10/15/07

"Did you not take a break?" I asked as I re-entered the room.

"No, I just want to get all of this behind me. I did the time, now I just want to do my time." He said with a look of concern.

I could tell the break gave him time to calm back down. "What's eating away at you? Why you trying to turn yourself in on crime the police said has not been reported. Riddle me that... That part... I am failing to comprehend."

"I told these police I wanted to turn myself in, they all laughed at me each time I came here. They called me a few days ago and told me they wanted me to speak with an investigator. So here I am."

His demeanor bothered me. But, it also gave me indications there was something bothering him and he didn't want to spill the beans on it. So I asked, "Give me more information about this group you 'sort of' joined. What was the benefits of being in it?

He hesitated and began looking around. "Please, what you think this is, the First 48? I can assure you there is no Hi-Tech camera system in here." Word play is a mug, yes there is a camera system but it's so old and outdated. I made a power move to get him to talk. "What I do have is a recorder in my bag, for my protection and evidence. I will sit my bag in the other room and we will continue this investigation."

"Ok, I can appreciate that." I grabbed my bag and stepped out the door. I called one of the officers over. I purposely stood by the window so Mr. Ian was able to see me handing the bag off to the officer.

I re-entered the room, took my seat and stated. "Ok, now let's talk... OTR." I learned in training that nothing is really off the record; it's one of the biggest lies to get information. Just like the lie about the recorded in my bag.

"What is OTR?" He asked.

"It means Off The Record." I answered as I anticipated information.

He began to tell me how the group was like a grown up Frat. It was a group of guys that didn't hate women, but they want to let women know men are the dominate species. He chuckled and paused a few times as he was giving me information about the group. He explained one of their saying were men shouldn't get into a relationship; it was said they should fuck em, feed em and forget them. Not always in that order. He also explained there was an initiation to get into the group and he told me the group name E.P.A.R stood for Eating Puss At Random. As we conversed, I could see he was opening up to me once again.

"So tell me, what role does this group play that you're sitting here trying to turn yourself in? I still don't get it." I asked firmly.

"Ok, remember how I was telling you there was an initiation? We had to break into a woman house and made sure she was at a discomfort without physically hurting her. It was a way to send a message that men are still powerful." He dropped his head in shame.

"So, what all did you do when you broke in the house? I asked hoping he would give full details.

He leaned back and started scratching the back of his head and said. "See, what had happened was..."

"Oh ummm ummm, I see we not being real with each other. I know when a sentence starts with 'what had happen' it is never what happened. I'm about to get my recorder back. We're going back on the record.

I stood up, he grab my hand. He had a gentle touch; his hands were like working man hands that were made to touch the gentle spots of a woman. "Hold on, there is no need. But, I need to know that you will not expose this group of the information I have provided to you."

I sat back at my seat and answered, "You have my word."

He went on and told me, "I'm not a stalker or anything; I was doing it to be a part of this group. The night I actually build up my nerves to break in I was drunk. I kind of remember the neighborhood but I have tried to find the house, but I can't remember exactly which house it was. All I know is I cut the alarm and phone lines and entered the house, I sat on the floor and I think I fell asleep for about fifteen minutes. I knew it was wrong and I began to feel wrongness in heart. I was going to just leave the house, but on my way back to the door she walked down the hall. Her body wasn't the best but what she was wearing was enticing. She stood about 5'5 a little less than average build caramel complexion chocolate woman."

"Oh wow, what did you do at that point?" I asked.

"My first thought was to just run out the house, but either way by now I know she was going to call the cops. It's strange though, she was wearing this shear covering. The covering was pulled closed. I could see her nipples were erected as she stood there asking me what I was doing in her house."

"So you mean to tell me you break in a dark house and could see this lady nipples? Really... A nipple?" I began to discredit his story.

"No I could. She had night lights all over the house. Even the panties she were wearing they were a pink and I could see through them. I could see was shaved down there and she left a trail of hair. It's what guys called a happy trail."

I rolled my eyes, but was wowed that he noticed all of that. I didn't think guys paid attention to the little things like that women do to turn them on. "So you were just standing there undressing her?"

"There was no need. I kind of felt like I was being seduce to be honest. She seem like she was expecting someone, they didn't show up and I was the stand in. It's just she was so calm to wake up to someone that has broke into her house."

"So, what stopped her from calling the police?"

"I stopped her. I ran up on her, placed my hand over her mouth wrestled her to her room, forced her on the bed and tied her mouth with pillow cases. I noticed there was an empty bottle of Red Wine. I took the sheets and tied her legs and feet. I was sure they weren't going to hold forever, but at least until I finished rummaging through her room. I started going through her room, looking for nothing, but just watching her to put the fear in her. I felt the wrongness and told myself I wasn't cut out for this. And it was strange because she didn't seem as alarmed as I thought she should have been. After I finished going in and out of her drawers I left. I have had this guilt on me since."

"Don't try and play all innocent like you noble, you have wronged this lady. You luck she haven't called the police and reported it. You could rack up all kind of charges."

"I wish she would just call the police." He said under his breath, but I heard him and acted like I didn't.

"Ok, now I have this information I will start my investigation and see if there are any reports of break ins. Can you write down the streets you think the house was on so I can ask the neighborhood watch?"

He obeyed and wrote down streets. I got his contact information and concluded our questioning.

"Excuse me ma'am. I am a private investigator. I heard from the Neighborhood watch there have been break-ins in the area. Do you know anything about this or have you heard anything about them?"

"I'm sorry; can you show my some proper ID?"

"Sure, my name K.I.T and as I said I am investigating break-ins in the area." I handed her my ID.

"Nice to meet you K.I.T, my name is Trinity. I have heard there were, but I don't really talk with the people around here. I kind of keep to myself."

"I notice there are some lines dug up on the side of your house. What happen there?"

She looked at me with the side eye. "I was out doing yard work a few months ago and I accidently cut the phone lines. I had a contractor come out, but they did a half ass job. They didn't even cover the lines back up. Good work is so hard to find."

"I know what you mean. You have a nice day and keep an eye out for suspicious activities."

"I will do that, K.I.T it was, right?"

"Yes, hope to be speaking with you soon."

Knock.. Knock.. Knock at the door. "Who is it?"

"Your Honor, this is me. Teliber. I have the P.I that wanted to speak with you about getting the clearance."

"Just one moment." Keys unlocking the doors to the chamber as K.I.T and Teliber walked in and took a seat.

"So I hear you want me to grant you a warrant to go inside a lady house that you assume her house was broken into by a guy that has been trying to turn himself in, but the offender never reported the crime. Is this correct?" The judge asked.

"That is correct your honor." I responded. Hoping the judge would see this in my favor.

"Well ma'am, it don't just work like that. I will not sign off on that but I will tell you, most people don't read the warrants when you present it them and even if they do they don't check to see if the signature is legit. "

"Oh really? So you saying I have a pass to enter her house... For work purpose that is." I could see how the judge was looking at me.

"All I am going to say is, if this comes up in court I will not vouch for you. I will not tell you how to get around the loop holes of the law, but if it comes up I will cover my ass and fry yours if that's the case."

"Thank you your honor, I think."

"You are welcome K.I.T. You're going to be a fine P.I. don't get so consumed in these cases you forget about your personal life. Leave work at work."

"Good advice Your Honor, thanks for everything."

"Not a problem, I am sure I will need you for something down the line."

I pulled up to the residence of Trinity. This was the weekend before Halloween, I did not want to have to present this fake warrant to her, so I came up with the game plan to wait it out until she leave the house and force my way in. The first break-in she didn't report, so I am going to. Normally the Friday before Halloween people would go to a Halloween party, so I was just going to camp out until she leave. Just my luck she was walking out the door minutes after I pulled up. It was already dark out so I wasn't too worried with anyone seeing me. I pulled my car around the corner to a vacant house and walked back up to her house.

I made it to the front door and to my surprise the door was open. I entered the door and started to look around the rooms. The house was neat; I went to the bedroom and found a box that was labeled Pandora. opened the box and there was a book in the box. I pulled the book out and realized it was a journal. I started reading the stories in the book. The first story in the book was dated back to August 22, 2007, I notice this date was similar to the date Mr. Ian was telling me he broke into her house and it read:

Trails of broken glass lead to a room lit by a night light upon a darken house.
Wrongness roamed the room as her pleasurable unpleasant moans cut through her pains of struggle. ADT was breach as he forced his way into her house and opening her box that Pandora had locked. Sheets were used to tie her to the bed, kicking and screaming as his massive hands controlled her spreaded legs, he punctured her piercing using his saliva a lubrication. She fought as long as she could, but that bottle of Red Wine she downed earlier calmed her as he repeated thrusting penetration. She wrapped her legs around him and sqirmingly arched her back as if she was trying to block his entrance. His deep tration felt moisture each time

he entered and a gripping during his outrance. He could have sworn her body was giving him an invitation. As the excitement for him fell, her moisture granted him to swell, her moans began to dwell...

Did he rape her, was my first thought. I had to close the book and gather my thoughts together. I was getting moist reading that story; I was thinking I need to have a couple rape rounds with Mr. Ian. Then I began to think, he told me the name of the group was E.P.A.R, that spells RAPE backwards. But if he raped her why didn't she report it? So I open the book again and started reading another story that was from September 5, 2007. This was a poem and it read:

Sheets crumbling from open and shut excited hands
thrusting me back and forth as he held his stallion stance.

My arms reaching were reaching for infinity
with spreaded finger as manly muscle enhanced.

Gripping of covers pulling them over my head
not wishing I was dead, once again being touched by a man.

I left all the windows cracked just a little this time
made sure he hit it from behind, bet he wondering how
I knew his name was Dan.

At this point I was confused. It seem like there was another break in. Did he break in several times or was there another one. I flipped through the pages of the book and there was 2 more dates with stories. I'd already spent enough time in this lady house so I didn't have time to read the rest of the stories. I took pictures of the pages and dates for evidence.

"Hey K.I.T, I got your message about meeting you here around lunch time. What was so urgent?"

I reached in my bag and pulled out a stack of papers. "This is why Mr. Ian." I stated as I dropped the papers on the table.

He fingered through he papers and asked, "What is this?"

"This is evidence that you raped lady house you broke into. Now I see why you were trying to turn yourself into the Police." It was hard for me to stand there and converse with him about that incident without getting aroused. That story I read, the things he was doing and how he was doing it to her. Something about the element of not knowing sprinkl with the unknown and forceful penetration kid of aroused me.

"Hold on there, I didn't rape anyone. She wanted it; I'm telling yo she was stimulated by this. She had an orgasm at least 3 times."

"So you did have sex with her?"

"Fuck." He yelled after realizing he just confesses.

"Dummy, don't you know there are women that don't need emotional attachments to have an orgasm. Their body will react to penetration and will reach a climax." I gave him the 'Don't Tell Me How a Female Body Operate' look. "Its funny you didn't say anything about you had sex with her when you gave me your 'OTR" down at the police station. "

"Fuck, fuck, fuck. I didn't rape her. "He yelled. I looked around and notice people were looking at us.

I replied. "After giving it some thought. I realized the organization name is Rape spelled backwards. But why didn't she didn't report it and charge you with rape."

"The bitch crazy."

"Excuse me. You may be facing rape charges and you calling your rapee crazy?" Even though I was thinking something was a lil weird with her, I had to stand up for my women.

"This bitch... I tell ya, this bitch is Psycho. Every since that night. I have been getting random phone calls about me coming back over and fucking her. She telling me how she never knew she liked to be tied up and taken advantage. She popped up at my job several times. She has broken into my apartments. I moved into a Co-Ed shelter and woke up one morning and she was standing over me. I had to move to an all men shelter to get a good night sleep. She even text me in Morse Codes one time asking me to make a molding shape of my dick so she can always have it with her. Who the fuck has that much time to learn how to text in Morse Codes?"

I was at awe. I was loss for words. "So you mean to tell me, you broke in her house, sexually assaulted/raped her, she enjoyed in and she stalking you?"

"I changed my number and threw that phone away. I felt like she had a tracker or something on it. Look I went and bout me a basic ass flip phone. See." He extended his hand out to show me the phone but all I could think about is the dick must be that good. For her to go to that extreme, WTF Mr. Ian knows?

"So that's why you trying to turn yourself in, it make sense now." I said as I started to gather my things.

"Yes!" He replied abrasive. "Every fucking time I went to the Police, they made a joke out of it and told me to grow a pair of balls. Those big nut, low testosterone donut eating and coffee drinking fuckers would not help me. So now you have the story, how are you going to help because I need to get back to work."

"I will be in touch." Those were my words, but not my thoughts as I walked away.

I spent the next few days investigating the E.P.A.R organization and found out they are a bunch of guys that have been hurt by women and feel they have been stripped of their manpower. So their mission is to draw in as many men as they could. I also found out the initiation was true and they have a guy inducted about twice a month.

I dug up some info on Mr. Ian, I found out his late wife said she was going out for a pack of cigarettes and a loaf of bread and never came back. (I know, so cliché. Writer couldn't think of any other scene than the loaf of bread and not return, oh well:) He found out she ran off to another country with older guy that was semi-rich. Her death was never determined and he has not been able to get closure on why she did it. So this group was an outlet for him.

Trinity was not that easy to get information on, she was fairly new to the city and her background was squeaky clean. I actually had to follow her around and leave some bread crumbs to for her to pickup. Low and behold, she took the bait and led me to be able to have a conversation with (Mr. Good Dick Ian, and Rape me Imma stalk you Trinity)!

I asked Mr. Ian to meet me at Rowlett Park. This was a fairly big park with plenty of activities. I tipped off Trinity that Ian would be there. I think she knew she was being lead there, but if was Mr. Ian was saying was true, she would not pass up an opportunity to see him.

I text Mr. Ian and told him I was running late, but I asked that he not leave. I sat in the park hours before he showed up and waited for Trinity to make her entrance. After two hours of wait time I had both of them in one place and I could finally get answers to un-asked questions.

As Trinity proceeded to the shelter Ian was sitting under. I greeted her. Ian had his back tuned and didn't see us walking up. She looked surprise, but she wasn't startled. "Good afternoon Dic." Trinity express.

"The name is K.I.T." I replied before giving it a thought she was referring to me as a detective.

"What brings you to this neck of the woods?" Trinity asked.

"I'm here for the same person you're here for, Trinity" I announced with an attitude.

"Oh, we have the same taste in men; I don't see a problem with that. I have learned to be open and try new things."

"Yeah, I have heard."

"Really, how much detail did he give you?"

"He gave me enough, but my question is why you never pressed charges?"

"Hey K.I.T, why you bring this deranged bitch with you." Mr. Ian stated as he walked upon us talking.

"Deranged, oh that's what I am?" Trinity responded.

"Yes, I have told you to stay away from me, but you keep coming back."

"I am trying to get you CUM Back to Back." She stated in her Drake mix tape voice.

"You need to stay the fuck away from me and keep my name out your mouth." Mr. Ian said as he point at her from afar.

"Out your mouth?" She replied. "You wasn't saying that when yo were E.P.A.R all up in my sauce."

I was standing there like a Ref, I was finally about to get the answers to the puzzle of rape or not rape.

"Yea girl, he join this lil group and I tell ya they are some feisty lil thangs."

"They" Mr. Ian and I replied simultaneously.

"Yes. They!" She replied looking at her nails. "I tell ya though Ian, you set the tone. When you were Eating my Pussy At Random I was glad it was my house you chose to break in that night."

E.P.A.R, all the time I was thinking the initiation was to rape someone, but it was really to eat random pussy. Wow. I looked over at Mr. Ian and shook my head. He had a look of shame on his face. I tuned back into her story.

"Girl let me tell you what the worthless man did." Trinity said while looking at me. "He broke in the house, sat down on the floor and fell asleep." I chuckled. "It woke me up, but it took some time for me to get up. I'd just downed a bottle of Red Wine. By the time I grab my gun and head to the back of the house, he leaning against the wall passed out. So now he is my prisoner.

"Oh wow." I replied as I was shaking my head thinking this some sick ish.

"I go the bathroom, freshen up and thrown on something sexy for intruder. On my way down the hall he gets up and proceeds to leave. I had to call him to get his attention. He turns around, after he undressed me with his eyes, and come towards me and places his hand over my mouth. He picks me up; I wrapped my leg around his back. I was in heaven. I hadn't had dick in months."

"I told you this bitch is sick. Who does shit like that?" Mr. Ian asks K.I.T.

"Let her finish." K.I.T replies. This was getting juice and I didn't want to miss a drop. For some time I forgot I was even on a case.

"He put me on the bed and started to tie me up and snatched my panties off. I never resist. I even actually turned a few times to make sure the knots were tight."

"Psycho bitch."

"Shush Mr. Ian." I replied.

"His hands, oh his hands. They melted my thighs every touch. I wasn't trying to close them as he was spreading them; I was just so sensitive that my body was reacting to his touch. He went in aggressively. He was slinging his tongue all over. He didn't miss a spot. He even took the time to run his tongue up and down my happy trail. I was being made love to, this wasn't an intruder rape, this was sheer and pure satisfaction."

I was speechless and was looking at Mr. Ian with the side eye. "Wow, he never told me that part of the story."

"You want details of how the penetration went?" Trinity asked with a grin on her face.

Thinking to myself, I already know but I didn't want to let her know how I knew. "Well you don't hav..."

"Oh yea, that's right." She interrupted me. "You already know."

I grew silent. I didn't know if she knew I broke in her house or not. "What do you mean?" I said with a croaking voice.

"Remember that day you came to my house and did the questioning? You recognized the wires were dug up. The installer had just finished running cameras in my house. All those little night lights you saw when you were in there, they were cameras."

"When I was in there?" I answered as if that statement was untrue.

"Yes." She replied. "When you were in there."

"What the fuck. Both you bitches are crazy." Mr. Ian said pointing at the both of us.

"Yes K.I.T." I saw you in my house, I saw you reading my journal and..."

I made a hard swallow, knew she wasn't going to spare me so I slightly tucked my chin in my shoulder.

"I saw you leaning back on my bed masturbating to the stories in the journal. I must admit, I got quite aroused and watched you getting off a few times."

I was so embarrassed. "Yep, you bitches are sick." Mr. Ian stated.

"Look like you need some good dick... DIC" She says as she stares at Mr. Ian crotch.

"Can you just leave me alone? That's all I ask of you." Mr. Ian asked.

"Under one condition, you convince this Dic to have a threesome with us. I promise to not press charges, I promise to not report the fake ass warrant you got K.I.T, plus you both have to promise to not expose the E.P.A.R organization."

Threesome, I'd never done that before and never intended. But the thought of having a run with Mr. Ian is making me lean towards it. Plus, I can stand to take the hit of unlawful entry on my first case. "You said early "THEY" were there more guys and how did you find out?

"When Ian left, he dropped a paper that had some written information on it. I did my research, found the organization and threaten to go public with it if they didn't give me the information I wanted. The guy told me how it worked, gave me Ian information and I have vowed my silence. But, you read the other stories; those were guys that joined after Ian. I wrote the poems and stories from the perspective of the guy, and how they would have worded it if they wrote it.

"Damn!" I expressed.

"Well, both you have my address. Let me know when we will be having the fun night. Time is limited." She said as she walked back to her car.

I reported the information gathered back to the Police Department. I provided them with details of the break in and how they came to an agreement. I didn't give details on the arrangement of the agreement. The Police department was happy with my work and they were finally able to close the case.

Ian was happy he was not being stalked and could go on with his life and not have to look over his shoulder all the time.

Trinity, well I guess she still prowling the guys from the E.P.A.R group and getting her a variety of sextitude.

Well I still have my job, so you know what that means and what took place. As far as for the detail with Mr. Ian that is **My 2nd Case** ;)

My Alleged Case

My Alleged Case

Veronica Trial

"It was you my heart looked upon, the lonely nights I needed to be caressed!" Those were the words Veronica whispered to herself as she took the stand. She raised her right hand and swore in to the Judge.

This was her comfort line when she was stressed or pressured. It was a line from her late husband poem titled <u>Blessed</u>. Veronica, Hispanic decent, grew up in a diverse culture. She was surrounded by many nationalities. She saw people for the person they were until she made it to Middle School. She has always had a thicker body build, never was she a runway model. In Middle School she was tease by kids about her weight, but later in life the same kids (boys and girls) came around with compliments and a blatant agenda due to her shape. Her long semi-curly hair, slightly slanted eyes and not so straight, but pearly white teeth that made her easy on the eyes plus a pretty smile. Yet, she still walked around with insecurities from being tease in Middle School.

"Mrs. Sheppard, you want to tell us what happen the night of the incident?" Judge asked in a kind voice.

"I am sitting here on this stand huh? I raised my right hand huh? Why would I be here if I didn't want to tell what happen that night? Huh?" Veronica said with attitudes as she looked in the direction of Judge.

"What the fuck?" The Judge said in a low high pitch tone as she rose up and drew her attention towards the Bailiff. "Is she talking to me?"

Judge Hall judges each case as an individual. She had a wealthy upbringing, but was exposed to a lot of White and Blue Collard crimes that often got swept under the rug. She became a Judge to help put away criminals, no matter their race, ethnic or how much money they have in their accounts. Although, she can be a little rough around the edges. Maybe seeing all the cases over the years takes a toll.

"Your Honor, my client is disturbed and has been this way since the incident. We tried to warn your cabin that it's best my client doesn't take the stand." Veronica well dress lawyer spoke up for Veronica.

"Oh no I'm just fine." Veronica interrupted the attorney. "I'm just fine. That bitch just need to learn her place and step back in line. "Where I'm from..." She then whispered. "We don't like your kind."

The courtroom went in a rage. The judge started coming out her robe and headed toward Veronica.

She was restraint by the Bailiff as she yelled to Veronica. "You're the one on trial here. I can make this three day trial end in three hours. One swing of this gavel and this shit is over for you. You murdered your husband and I hope you rot in jail the rest of your LIFE." Even though Judge Hall took an oath to not allow her personal opinions to have an effect on her cases, Veronica touched a nerve.

Every mouth in the court dropped. Speechless became the new silence, and then Veronica spoke. "LiFe. You think that's what this is? My life died a year ago with my husband. Since then, I took the F out life and fuck myself with it every day knowing I'm living a lie." She stood up, leaned over the stand and directed her speech to the Judge. "That mother fucker slowly started sending his clothes from the house to another country. He started having private conversations. He was getting ready to leave me." Her demeanor went from anger to danger as she finished her speech. "You know what else happen?" Her Attorney walked towards her. "When I found those airline tickets."

"Don't you say it." Her Attorney spoke.

"I waited for him to come in from work."

"Don't you fucking say it." The attorney expressed.

"I dropped my robe with nothing under it"

"Veronica no." He looked at her."Don't do this to yourself."

"He took off all his clothes."

"Don't fucking do it." He pleaded.

"I pulled the hammer back on the revolver"

"Nooooooooooo." He screams as he pounded his fist on the table.

"And I took the life he was taking from me. BOOM..."

"Fuck!" The lawyer said as he dropped his head.

The Incident

"Hey Veronica, I called you back as soon as I saw the message. Is something wrong? Everyone O.K? You never text me, you always call and leave a message. I know if you take the time to send me a text something must be really serious. I couldn't imagine what I would do if something happened to you or... "Veronica stopped her frantic friend in mid-sentence.

"Shawnie, calm down. Girl you gone work my nerves and upset me more than I am now." Veronica spoke as she tried to calm herself down.

"I'm sorry, I just get. You know I just. It just seem like you were. Well, you know." Shawnie said as the seat belt reminder was constantly sounding, reminding her to buckle up.

"Girl, where you heading? Shouldn't you be at work until 10 tonight?" Veronica asked.

"After I saw your text, I told my Superior that I needed to leave and I would explain when I make it back." Shawnie stated as she continued to drive.

"Oh Shawnie, let me give you the Tea about your brother Paul." Shawnie and Veronica have been friends since they were knee high to a grasshopper. They had wild college nights, cried on each other shoulders through rough breakups and even share memories from a night at a Swingers Party that almost cost Veronica her marriage.

"Veronica, you know Paul would kill me if he knew you were coming to me about yall marriage. You remember how hard he was on me the last time I got into yall business. I'm not up for that again."

"But, Shawnie it's not me this time. I have hard core evidence. He has a flight, a passport and even an apartment in another country. He has it in a fake name. Passport and all. He so dumb, he used the name he always use when he writing them exotic poems and stories. He even has a woman's name on the other ticket and a passport for her but no picture."

"Veronica, you not going to put me in this. Not this time. I am about to take my black ass back to work. You know my financial struggle, I need all my money. I thought there was something seriously wrong. That's yall marriage, so yall deal with it the best way yall know how."

"But Shawnie, he has not touched me in months. I hear him on phone making plans that don't involve me. You know since that last incident I have giving Paul my all." Shawnie could hear the cry in her voice. She knew she was hurt but she was not going to get involved in it this time.

"Veronica, I know you're hurt and you are in your feelings. Talk to Paul, it may not even be what it seem. Talk to your husband about your issues and concerns. I can no longer be that person. I will call and check up on you tomorrow. Talk to your husband when he make it in tonight, and listen to what he has to say!" Shawnie hung up the phone with a clear heart.

For the next few hours Veronica replayed scenes in her head. She allowed her anger to get the best of her. She believed the man she once loved lifelessly has falling out of love with her and was about to move forward without her. Although they had their rights and wrongs in their marriage, she couldn't see them living separate lives with other people. So when Paul made it home she did the unthinkable thoughts she'd rehearse the past few hours.

Keys rattling at the door, she knew it was her husband coming home for the night. "Here honey, I poured you a glass of wine." She extended the glass as she greeted him at the door.

"Thank you Nica." Nica was a nick name he gave her since they were kids. He too was one of the kids that picked on her back in Middle School, but he told her he really liked her and that was the only way he knew how to get attention from her.

Paul was a scruffy looking white guy. He was that white guy that grew up on the other side of the tracks. He had to work and help his mom and disable father maintain bills since he was a kid. He was a really creative and quite intelligent guy. He stood about five foot eleven inches just over two hundred pounds with a freckled looking complexion. He aged well and still had a youthful look. It was hard to catch him is a suit, but when he did, he cleaned up really well.

"What did I do to have the pleasure of this treatment? I see you wearing the robe I like." Paul said as he took a sip of the wine.

"Oh really, your favorite robe? I didn't know you even notice. Would you like to see what I have on under it?" She said as she slow strutted way from him walking towards the kitchen counter.

Before he could answer, she untied the robe and let it fall to the floor as she continued to walk. She turned around to reveal her nakedness. She watched the wine glass slip from his hand and fall to the floor. The glass scattered on to the floor, Paul stood in shock with his mouth open and his hand still cupped as if he was still holding the glass.

"You better close that mouth of yours, I may put something in it that later can't be explain." Veronica added.

"Oh, shit. The floor, the glass, the glass hit the floor. I was... I was... I..." Paul was lost for words. He couldn't complete his sentence.

"Oh honey. You acting like this is your first time seeing this. This yours for the remainder of your life."

"I know honey. I just... I was just caught off guard." He said as he leaned down to pick up the broken glass.

"Oh Paul, you are such a dear. Leave that glass for now I will have some other cleanup a little later. Come here, I have something for you." She said as she leaned against the counter propping one of her legs on the barstool exposing her clean shaved private parts.

Paul put the pieces he had in his hand in the garbage and walked towards her. "I have been attracted to you every since we were little kid I remember the first time I saw you naked. I felt that same feeling just now when you walked out of that robe. All these years and you still have that affect on me."

She began to fall into the pity of his words and word play. She then realized, he is a writer. Words like that are easy for him. She responded, "That's a nice suit. You only wear one for our Anniversary or funeral. Today is not our Anniversary, so is there a funeral?"

"Funny you asked, I been wanting to talk you about this thing I had in mind. I met with some people tonig..." She put her finger over his mouth and stopped him from completing his sentence. She could feel h was about to feed her cow size load of bull shit.

"Take it off, right now. All of it. Even socks and draws." She request authoritatively.

"Granted." He replied as he began to remove cloth one layer at a time. She reached over counter and picked up the folder that contained passport and apartment information. "I'm naked, now what? He asked as he did the "Drop the Mic" motion with his underwear.

She slid the folder over to his direction and she asked, "What the fuck is this shit Paul?" She asked as she lifted the napkin and pulled out the revolver and pointed it at him.

"Whoa, baby. Put the gun down and let's talk about this. I was gonna..." She pulled the hammer back on the gun.

"You were going to do what, leave me? Paul you were going to leave me?? After all we have been through. You about to go and do this to me?"

"It's not like that Nica. Put the gun away and let me explain what's happening here." Paul says as he slow lifts his hand toward the gun.

"There is nothing to explain here." Veronica voiced as she began to back away from him with the gun still pointed at him. "All the proof I need is right in that folder. If I can't have you I won't let anyone have you." She said as she lowered the gun towards his penis area.

"Nica please don't do this. I am sorry for keeping this a secret from you. I promise, let me explain and it will all make sense. It's not what it seem, just let me explain."

"I came to you the last couple months and told you I have not been happy. You have not responded to none of my cries. I cry in the shower almost every day. Where the fuck are you when I am here crying? Out fucking some other bitch." She spoke in a rage poking the gun at him while she crying.

"Whoa honey. That's not true. Let's talk about this, please put the gun down." He said nervously.

She dropped her head in silence for a moment. She then lift her head, closed her eyes and said, "I love you Paul and I always will."

"Nica please!!!!!!!" He yelled just before she started pulling the trigger. She reported after she pulled the trigger the first time, her adrenaline took over and she is not sure how many times she actually shot.

April 3, 201.
5:57an

"Good morning Mrs. Sheppard, my name is KIT. I am the private investigator that is assigned to this case. I know you may have been questioned by several different people, but if you are not willing to answer any questions right now. I can understand."

"I am sorry KIT. I am too tired of all the questions. I just need some time to process all of this."

"I can respect that and understand it Mrs. Sheppard. Here is my card, if you have any questions are ready to talk please don't hesitate to call me."

"I don't know if you notice KIT, but I am in custody. I am not sure how I would be able to just give you a call from jail."

"Mrs. Sheppard if you let any of the officers know that you are ready to speak on this, they will contact me. I assure you of that."

"Ok, one thing KIT. They say I shot my husband in the leg. How die he die from that? And how did they pronounce him dead so fast? That's something you may need to investigate."

"I am sorry Mrs. Sheppard, but I am not a medical specialist and I cannot answer any of those questions for you. But, you know your husband better than anyone else. I'm sure you know he did everything for your best interest. My apologies go out to you and his family for his absences. Always remember, it is you his heart look upon."

Veronica just put her head back down on the desk as KIT and the other officer's exits the room.

****

The Explanation

"Good morning Mr. Sheppard, thanks for meeting me on out of the office. This is not something I want to get out." Marcus asked as he surveyed his surroundings.

"No problem, I am grateful you're willing to work with us on this." Paul said as he extended his hand to close the handshake.

"This must be the wife." Marcus asked.

"No, this is not my wife." Paul said as he looked away. There was moment of awkward silence. This is my sister Shawnie. "Shawnie, meet Marcus. He is from Life Changers Inc."

"Nice to meet you." Shawnie said as she gave a quick wave.

"Oh, ok." Marcus said with confusion in his tone as he waved back.

"Oh no, I have not told the wife yet. I want to make sure everything is a go before I go to her with it. My sister and my wife are best friends; I had to let my sister in on it so I am not being question by my wife and my sister while this put in place."

"Ok, cool." Marcus responded as he continued explaining the details about the apartment overseas. He explained he have a connectio at the airport on both sides. He told him who he needed to contact whe he and his wife plan on taking the flight. He also explained once they leave they can never return to the United States.

Paul explained to Shawnie that he made a deal with the Devil and he is not able to satisfy his end of the deal. They gave him 1 year to satisfy his end of the deal. He explained to her he needed to leave the Country. He explained he got new identifications for him and Veronica. He made her vow to not say anything to Veronica about this and he would forgive her for the incident that took place months earlier. Shawnie agreed to keep her silence until the plan was fully developed.

****

The Confrontation

"Look Shawnie, there he goes. He getting out the car to and heading to that restaurant." Veronica said in anger.

"I see him girl. Let's get out and get a little closer. You know you will have to walk up on him and tap him on the shoulder while he doing wrong to make him admit to it." Shawnie said as they headed into the restaurant.

"And that is exactly what I am about to do." Veronica said as she headed towards the table where Paul and the lady sat.

"Veronica, calm down and take a deep breath before you go ove there. You know you have anger issues and sometimes you go overboard." Shawnie said as she followed swiftly.

"Oh, you haven't seen overboard." Veronica stated as they approached the table.

"Wife, what you doing here?" Paul said in a startling voice.

"What's this shit Paul?" Veronica voiced as she pointed at the lac sitting at the table.

"This is Tiffany; she works with Life Changers Inc." Paul explained as he saw the expression change on Tiffany face.

"Well, she about to have a Life Changer in this Incorporation."

Veronica said as she reached across the table and grabbed Tiffany by her hair.

"Nica, what the hell." Paul shouted as he watched a fist fly by his face and lands on the ear of Tiffany.

"Veronica, stop. You going to get yourself in trouble." Shawnie said as she made an attempt to pull her away from Tiffany.

Veronica shot a quick elbow to Shawnie chest that dropped her to the floor. She let Tiffany hair go, took a boxer hop backwards, planted her back foot and leaned in with a crossed the body jab followed by a left hook. Both landing on the face of Tiffany.

Tiffany face planked the table as she was out cold. Paul jumped up and wrestled Veronica to the floor. He looked up at his sister with disgust as he held his wife on the floor. The restaurant security and the Police showed up as the on-lookers stood around awaiting other actions.

Veronica was cuffed and taken to the station. The officer explained that she would have to be booked and the attackee has 24 hours to press charges. If no charges are pressed they will release her on her own recognizance.

Paul apologized to Tiffany as she left in the Ambulance. He and Shawnie stood out front of the restaurant as the Ambulance left with Tiffany and the Police took Veronica to the station.

"Sis, you happy now? First you take my wife to a Swingers Club, now this? You still upset that I married your best friend? You need to get over that and stop trying to sabotage my marriage. You need to stay the fuck out of our business."

Shawnie wasn't happy when her best friend and brother started dating. There were too many things she knew about both of them and didn't feel they were a good fit for each other. "First of all, when we went to that club you and Veronica was not married. Second of all she was my friend before you even started dating her. Third of all, you are sabotaging your marriage by having this secret lunch with women without your wife knowing. Lastly, I am not in your business. Look around bro, you making your business public."

Shawnie did feel guilty and embarrassed for being a part of this blowup. As most humans, if you back them against the wall they find a defense mechanism to account for their wrong actions.

Paul turn to her and stated, "When Nica and I was just dating and yall had yall lil stake outs, following me around and popping up at places like the crew of Cheaters, that was one thing. But now, this is my wife. The person in which I will spend the rest of my life." He turned and looked into the skies. "I have never seen you as anything less than a sister. At the age of 7, the foster home came to me and told me I was going to be adopted by a black family that had a black daughter I was excited to finally have family." Paul began to tear up as he continued to speak. "Your mom... Our mom loved me like I was her very own. Our dad treated me like the son he always wanted. Even though they hit hard times and I had to go find a job to help out with the bills I didn't hesitate. He looked over to Shawnie and he could see her eyes filling up with tears. "I have always heard the saying that blood only makes you related and loyalty makes you family. I have been loyal to you as a sibling since I met you. Today, this stunt you pulled makes me feel like we are not related. You have no clue of what you all may have messed up for the future of me and my wife." Just before he walked off, he pointed at Shawnie and said. "Once again, get you some business and stay the fuck out of my marriage life.

Shawnie heart dropped two tectonic plates as he walked off leaving her with a heart filled with anguish, hurt and a forever scar. In her mind, if the two of them separate then she would have her old friend back, plus her brother. Until that moment she never realized she was fighting the wrong battle. Even if they separated they could never be the same person they were. She sat in her car and cried for hours. At that moment she understood how to be loyal to her brother and vowed to never interfere in his marriage.

* *

KIT Testimony

"KIT, that is what you preferred to be called right." Judge Hall asked.

"Yes your honor." KIT responded.

"So, with all this stuff you just told us about the Sheppard's, their families and friends, how can we validate what's true and what is being fabricated?" Judge Hall asked as she awaited a response.

"I have no dog in this fight." KIT responses as she hesitated and anticipated the next question. After her short pause she continued, "I was hired to do a job and that is what I did. I am simply reporting my findings. Your Honor," She ended that sentences with attitudes.

"Three years ago Veronica was sentenced to 5 years in prison for the murder of her husband with the possibility of Parole with good behavior. She took a plea that I am still questioning, but the jury concluded. What information you have that pertains to any of this?

"Under my investigation I found out Mr. Sheppard was working with a Company known as Life Changing Inc. They are known to give people a second chance in life. They help get careers started, finding new homes, and getting people out of battered environments and also they have safe houses in which they will place people in protected custody." KIT was explaining before she was interrupted.

"How is all of this in relations to the murder?" Judge Hall asked.

"Well you see." KIT said as she positioned herself be detailed. "Mr. Sheppard had a few meetings with staff members out of the company office. One of the meetings was with a Tiffany Hindsburg. She controls the financial arrangements for the Life Changing. Their first meeting ended with her being hospitalize by Mrs. Sheppard. After that encounter Mr. Sheppard had to renegotiate his contract being they saw this as a bigger risk. They reassigned his case to Marcus Invictus. He handles the "High Profile" cases. Marcus and Mr. Sheppard worked together for months on this case; they'd finally got everything in place. Marcus told me Mr. Sheppard was so excited and couldn't wait to get home and break the news to his wife. He was finally about to get away for the people that were extorting him and his family."

"Look like he got away forever." Judge Hall stated. "I'm concern KIT; you said you don't have a dog in this fight. Why are you sharing all this information three years later?"

KIT leaned forward. "My job is to investigate and make sure the proper information is being presented. I know there are detectives out there that just need something close enough. They don't need all the details, they will make their case on only the information they have. It took me three years to get to the bottom of this and get all the information of this case. I like to sleep well at night knowing I did all and gave my all. To know a lady is sitting in jail for murdering her husband when that is really not the case, I can't sleep well knowing there is other evidence out there."

"What are you saying KIT? You don't think she murdered her husband? She stood before a jury and said she pulled the hammer back and BOOM. She took the life from him that he was trying to take from her. If I stand correct, those were her exact words." Judge Hall stated as she closed the files she was reading.

"Your honor, Mr. Sheppard was shot in the leg, no main organs were hit. He was pronounced dead before making it to the hospital. His wife was not allowed to confirm the body. They had a cremation and no viewing for his body." KIT explained.

"Oh, so you're a Private-I and a Doctor now?" Judge Hall expressed.

KIT chuckled. "No your honor, I am not. But, through my investigation, I learned the people that transported Mr. Sheppard after the shooting were paramedic on the payroll of the Life Changing. His body was taken to and exchanged with a person that was already dead that resembles his description."

"Well, how do you explain the Deoxyribonucleic acid that was used to verify the person they had in their possession? Doctor KIT!" Judge Hall said with aggression.

"The what? I'm not sure what you're asking. I have never heard that word a day in my life." KIT stated in confusion.

The judge leaned forward; "That is my point exactly. You are not Doctor KIT, you are an investigator. That is the scientific term for DNA. Stay in your lane Dic... I mean KIT."

"I see Dic is just the running joke for a P.I huh." KIT says under her voice.

"Excuse me ma'am I didn't hear that last remark." Judge asked.

"Oh nothing I was just talking to myself your honor." KIT felt like the smallest pea in the pot after not knowing the proper term for DNA. She knew she had to recover to be able to present all the information she'd discovered the past three years. "So your honor, that was a great question and very informative how you educated myself and I am sure a few more people in this Court Room the meaning of DNA. But, to answer you; Mr. Sheppard made trips to the dentist and had all of his teeth removed. He got them replaced with dentures. And if I recall in the report, they verified his Deoxyribonucleic acid through his dentures."

Giggles and rumble started to stir up in the court. KIT felt like she worked her way back into the battle. "Silence in the court." Judge Hall requested. "KIT, so you're saying the shooting that landed Mrs. Sheppard in jail was all staged. You saying this is all a setup. You're telling me these people knew she was going to shoot her husband and they were just on a standby and waiting to get the call for the shots? Mr. Sheppard testified and verified she spoke with Mrs. Sheppard the night of the shooting. We have phone records to back the testimony. His sister has been in therapy since the day the person you claim is sitting in jail for something she didn't do. What kind of evidence you have to hack this up?"

"All I'm saying is I found out there were a lot of people on payroll when all of this happened. I know Mrs. Sheppard attorney was funded by Life Changing. I know over half of the Jury or even all of them were funded by Life Changing as well. Also, I am questioning a payment that was presented to your husband around the time of the trial."

Judge Hall looked over at the Bailiff and asked. "Isn't that slander, or treason. Did she accuse me of treason? KIT, I think you are a good person at heart and I think you may even be good at your job at times. You're over your head on this one KIT. Did anyone tell you that Mrs. Sheppard was found dead in her cell over a week ago? She hung herself, no note or anything. She was smart about it, she did it right after shift change and after the guard did his first round.

KIT dropped her head in shame, you can see the pain and how embarrassed she was, "I am sorry. My condolence goes out to the family."
"Thank you for your compassion. If there are no further statements, we will have the closing statements."

Court adjourned and no new information was input on this case. They gave Veronica a proper burial and no one really spoke about the case ever again.

The Alleged

One day while gathering my things to take on another case. I checked flipped over a post card from Amsterdam. The postcard picture displayed a painting for Van Gogh and the elaborate Canal system. Looking at the picture reminded me there are people that free from the woes of this world. And the post card read:

Hey KIT,

There is no way we could ever repay you for what you have done for us. I know there were some hard nights and days of investigating, looking through paper work and processing files. The many court appearances and family interviews. Through it all KIT, you stood firm and you didn't crack under pressure. That last court appearance was a phenomena performance. If you are ever up to visit a great County to see the artistic heritage that is offered in the Netherlands, we will surely arrange that for you. You did a great job getting my wife up to par. For years she was clueless. I thank you for all the hard work and effort you put into this. Once again we appreciate you KIT.

From,
You know who!

When I became a Private Investigator, there were two things I told myself I would not allow to take place. One was to have a relationship of any kind with clients, investigates of any law enforcement surrounding any case I work. Secondly, I said I would never take a bride for any reason being there is no dollar amount that would be worth withholding any truthful information. As far as this case, I told Judge Hall the truth, but she refuse to accept it. I read her like a book the first time we were in court; I knew once her case was closed, she didn't really want to have to dig it back up. I'm not saying I took a bride for this case, were going to say it is ALLEGED!

My Last Case

"Damn Blake. How you gone to pull this off with your wife? I just drained your ass of all your energy." Audrey said as she stretched her nakedness across the edge of the bed.

He looked over to her. He could see her stretch marks knowing the history of how she got them. Much like his Olivia, she didn't have any kids. He was grateful she didn't due to the life she lived. Her life consists of drugs, pain, suffering plus she came from a poverty environment that made it hard for her to survive. "Woman, you just don't know what I go through to spend this time with you." He replied in a gentle voice.

"I often ask myself why you do the things you do, but I always answer it with the question, if you didn't do these things, where would I be in life?" She said while curling up in the fetal position and clutching the sheets close to her body.

He crawled down to the end of the bed and he could see tears forming in her eyes, he could see she was trying to hold them back when he asked her… "You know why I do this?"

A smirk came upon her face because she knew what was coming next. She knew he was about to start quoting lyrics from a recording artist by the name of Platinum. He began reciting in a low whispering tone… "I do this for the pain, I do this for the hustle, I do this for my Audrey everyday with her struggles, I do this for your hood, and I do this for my hood… I do this cause I love you." They have been having an affair for over a year, but this was the first time he ever said he loved her.

She rolled over and drew his body close to hers; she pressed his face against hers. Not to give him a kiss, but she just wanted to inhale his exhale. She released a moan as she began to feel his manly swell. She thought she drained him the last round, but it's apparent there was still water left to sprout out of his whale. I'm sure the imagination will over exaggerate what really took place next, but "Oh Well!"

June 8, 2010 10:14am

"Good morning wife." Blake greeted her as she walked the kitchen. "Looks like that bed just wouldn't let you this morning huh?" I said to her. She walked over and retrieved the cup of coffee he made f her. "Olivia, are you not talking to me today?" He asked as he stirred tl eggs.

"Blake, do you think I am a fucking fool? I felt you sneaking in th bed this morning. I was just in the room making up the bed; I saw stran of hair that I know didn't come out of my head. You keep taking me to that Dr. like I am some kind of Psycho. He keeps giving me all these pill: like I am a fucking druggie. I have you know, I know when I take the meds and pass out, I know you sneaking out the house and running around with some lil hussy. That's why I haven't been taking them lately

Olivia was having a break down early in the morning. She began to hyperventilate and getting short of breathe. "Honey, you need to take your meds. If you keep this up you are going to pass out again. Yo remember you almost broke your arm the last time you fell out. You ne to be well for our two O'clock appointment with the Dr." He stated as h reached in the counter to get her injection.

"Ohhhh yeaaa. That's what you want; you want me to get all drugged up so I can run out the house and be with that other woman?"

"Honey, there is no other woman. It's only you. You have to tru me." He had guilt as he made that statement. Not because of the affaii but how attached he became to Audrey.

"The only thing you ever really do with me anymore is take me to see that Dr. Hope. What kind of name is hope? Is he even a real Dr? I hope one day I go there and he can tell me who the hell Audrey is. One night I was sucking yo dick and right before you came you call called me Audrey. Can you tell meeeee..."

Blake injected her with her meds that calm her from her panic attacks. He held her in his arms and rocked back and forth with her. He had thoughts of Audrey and how he enjoyed her company. Though he loved his wife and would not trade her, there were times he wished he could magically merge Audrey and Olivia, which would stop the tearing of his heart.

June 8, 2010 – 1:48pm

"Blake?"

"Yes Olivia."

"Do you love me?" Olivia asked as she buried her head in Blake chest as they waited to be called by the Dr.

"Yes." He paused before he continued. "Yes I do Olivia." He delivered his answer with sincere.

"You know I'm not well, some times worse than others, what's keeping you around? I know you say you love me, but over the last year our relationship has been declining." Blake didn't verbally entertain her comments or questions, but, he began to look over the past year and how it has changed. He knew Audrey was a distraction, but he also felt deep down that she was also a reminder why he loved Olivia so much. She continued her rant as he thought over his thoughts... "Blake, there are nights I have dreams, and in those dreams I can see you with this other woman. I can never really make out her face, but she kinda looks familiar."

"Baby, not now. Don't get yourself worked up before we go in and see the Dr."

"Every time I bring this up you try and shelter it. When is a good time to talk about it? Hell we rarely ever even talk anymore. Where is the fire and desire you promised me in our relationship? Baby do you ever hear my cries?" She expressed as she began to get emotional and tears began to form. "What is it you want me to do to get us back to us being us? Baby, can we just start this over and...

"Olivia and Blake Miller, please report to door number three. I repeat, Mrs. and Mr. Miller please report to door number three." Her rant was interrupted by the intercom.

They removed themselves from their chairs simultaneously and proceeded to the door. The meetings with Dr. Hope sometimes get extensive, personal and very intense. That's the reason why he always schedules them in the afternoon.

"Good afternoon Mr. and Mrs. Miller. How are thing going this week?" Dr. Hope asked as he welcomed them into his office.

Olivia looked over at Blake as she was still in her feelings from the unfinished conversation. "Week was fine "DR. HOPE" I guess." She stated as she symbolized quotation marks with her two fingers on each hand.

"We're doing well Doc. This week is still early, nothing out of the ordinary." He answers as he interlaces his fingers with his wife and looks over to her.

"Well that's good. Shall we get started?" They both proceeded t the designated couch available as they started the counseling.

Dr. Hope has been seeing the couple for the past year since Olivia's accident. Olivia worked for a Law Firm in a corporate building prior to the accident. It was reported she was taking the stairs instead of the elevator for a fitness month they were having at work. She slipped and fell down a couple flights of stairs. The Law Firm settled with her, paid her a pension and released her from the company.

"How have the meds been working, and have you been taking them as instructed?" The Dr. asked while looking through the charts.

"He won't even touch me." Olivia blurted. Dr. Hope and Blake looked at each other with confusion in their eyes. "I mean, yes. I have been taking them. DR." She stated while looking at Blake with the 'You better not say anything' look.

"Ok, moving right along." Dr. Hope stated.

The Dr. sat and spoke with the couple about their normal and usual process. He spoke to them about dealing with traumatic events and how it could impact the life of everyone around them. He gave them more exercises on communication and relaxations. After giving his pep-talk with the couple, Olivia was escorted out the room with the assistant to do her weekly testing and scanning. During this time is when Blake updates Dr. Hope with progression.

"So, Mr. Miller, how is the Erasure working out for you and her?" He asked with a concern.

"It's working for us, no concerns that I could pin point." Blake answered.

"Are there any side effects and/or changes you see? She has been on it for about a year now, anything different with her or does she ever recap on anything from the past?"

Blake began looking within himself. He thinking he has paid this Dr. to erase certain sections of his wife memory. He keeps telling himself he is doing it for the sake of her and him, but then he have those days he feel like he is the only one benefitting from it.

"Well Doc, she can remember there was a fall; she can remember some of the people she worked with at the firm, but the tragic behind the fall she never bring up, so that part I don't think she can remembers."

"Wait, so she can remember the people she worked with? Did she mention any names in particular? You know I am taking a risk doing this I could lose my practice."

"Yea I know and I thank you. She can remembers her boss, and I think she remember a few of her co-works. She mentions names of a few of the people, but I don't remember them."

"Oh, ok. She worked at a Law Firm right?"

"Yea." Blake answers with hesitation in his voice and a concern look.

"Did she happen to mention any of the clients she was involves with?"

"Involved with?" Blake answered defensively. "Da fuck?" He released as he sat up in his chair.

"No... No, no, no, no... I am, I mean. The clients she worked with." Silence became of them and the moment was awkward. "I'm sorry Blake... I know this is a hard time..."

"No, you good." Blake cut him off before he could finish his statement. "In a way, I prayed for this." He stated with his head buried in his hands.

After a few more moments in silence the ice was broken. The assistant brought Olivia back in the room. They went over her results and what she needed to look forward to in the next few visits. Dr. Hope shook Blake hand and gave Olivia a hug as he walked them to the receptionist desk.

July 17, 2010 9:26pm

"Wake up sleepy head. It's time for round two." Blake smiles and was being greeted by passionate kisses before he could even open his eyes. He could smell the alcohol from earlier on her breathe. He could taste the sweetness of the chaser on her bottom lip. "Can the whale cum out and play? I want to see how long it's going to take for me to make it sprout." Audrey stated as she kissed her way down his chest and abdominal crevasse.

"Oh yes Audrey, you know just what to do and when to do it." He kept his eyes closed, leaned back to enjoy the suction.

She began licking the side of his balls. She engulfed one of them in her mouth and then took her hand and gently plucked the other one. This wasn't a sexual sensation to him, but it gave his body an instant shock and it increased his blood flow. She watched his whale rise. She had him slide down to the end of the bed and plant his feet on the floor. She hopped in his lap and teased the top of his penis with the moist opening of her puss. With no hands she lined his dick so it was centered with her opening. She began kissing him behind his ear and making her was down to the back of his neck. She knew this was his spot and knew this would turn him on.

He reached around her waist with one hand to pull her down so he could penetrate her warm moist opening. She slapped his hand away and pushed him so he would be lying back on the bed. "Bad boy you are, so now you shall be punished."

"Ok." He answered with excitement as he awaited his punishment.

She slid down off the foot of the bed. She took his dick and pull it downward as his balls slightly hung off the bed. She positioned herse so she was able to indulge at least fifty percent of dick between her jaw She began sucking in a stroking motion. He could feel the tuck in her tongue as she got into her rhythm. On various strokes would push to force his dick to the back of her throat, just so she could nip his balls wit the tip of her tongue. He looked up and all he could see is the side of h wig going up and down. He could feel his penis stretching her jaws each time her head came up. He felt his blood gushing through his body, he could fell the tingling. He rose up like Cane from WWE and forced her locomotion to a halt. He stood up and forced her onto the bed. She wa lying on her stomach and she said, "Yes daddy, you know I like that ruff stuff."

He spread her legs as she was partial hanging off the bed with he feet planted on the floor. "Now you assume the fucking position."

"At your command." She whispers in her One Nine hundred voi just before he inserts her. They went at it for hours as if they took flight on a plane. The nearby neighbors may have not known them or even known their name, but if you'd walked passed that door that night you would have been like, they in there doing they thang.

July 18, 2010 1:45am

As Blake began to get out the car and head back to the house. H noticed a car that he has been seeing a lot in the past couple months. H rushed into the building; he pressed the button for the elevator and the hid in the stairwell and peep through the glass. He notices a young lady with a camera on her side. He watched her press the elevator and entered the elevator. He rushed up the stairs to the second floor where they lived. From the end of the stairwell he could see the door to their condo. He watched the young lady get off the elevator, walk down the corridor and then she slowed down as she passed his door. She took a couple steps and walked pass the door again. She repeated this step several times before she made her way back to the elevator.

Blake rushed down the stairs and waited outside by the young lady car. As she walked out the building he approached her. "Who the hell are you, and why the hell have you been following me?" Blake asked as he continue to approach her.

"Mr. Miller, wait. I can explain."

"Mr. Miller? How do you know my name? I'm going to ask you one more time, if you don't identify yourself it's gone to be a mid-night crime." He said as he pulled out his pistol and pointed it at her.

"My name is Kitana Lewis, I am a Private-I, my code name is KIT stands for Kept-In-The Dark, I was hired by your wife because she suspected infidelity." She stated all in one breathe.

They both began looking at the ground. "Did you just piss yourself?" Blake asked with a smirk on his face.

"Please don't shoot me sir. Please, I am a good person. I'm just doing my job sir."

"I'm not going to shoot you." He stated as he put his gun away. "But, you have to tell me everything you have found out.

He gave her his jacket to wrap around her waist and they headed to the nearby Diner. They sat and talk for a few hours. He learn what really happen with the fall at his wife job and her fall in the stairwell, he understood why it was so important to know who she remembered from her job. KIT showed him all the footage and notes she had. She questioned the wellness of his wife from the stuff she learned. Blake tried to get KIT to not report to his wife with her new findings, but KIT explained everything was pre-paid already by his wife and she will have to report everything. Blake thanked her for her time as they parted ways.

July 23, 2010 2:45pm

Blake was sitting in the Doctor's office waiting to see Dr. Hope. The appointment was at three o' clock, he had been sitting in the lobby since 2pm. "Blake Miller, please report to door number one. I repeat, Blake Miller please report to door number one.

Blake stood up, took out his cell phone, dialed 911 and placed the phone on the seat of the chair he was sitting. Blake walked into the office; he turned around and locked the office door, then he began walking towards Dr. Hope desk. "Dennis Hope. I know everything. Dennis." Blake stated as he rolled up his sleeve on his shirt.

"I have been waiting for you all week Blake." Dr. Hope stated as he pulled his gun out of his drawer.

He stood up and raised his gun and fired two shots hitting Blake in his chest. He lowered his gun as he watched Blake take two small steps back looking at the holes in his shirt. Blake yells, "Teflon, mutha fucker." As launched himself across Dr. Hope desk and wrestling him to the ground. Blake began to combine combinations of knuckles to face. "You took everything from us; do you even know what we went through? Mutha fucka I told you everything that was going on with us. That Erasure was to make sure your secret was safe, but guess what, the cat is out the bag and now it's time for you to pay."

Busy pounding away, Blake didn't notice Dr. Hope pulling out a knife. He stabbed Blake in the side. He drew back to stab Blake again when Blake picked up the gun and shot Dr. Hope twice in the chest.

Blake stood over him and moments later the Police was kicking in the door. Blake placed the gun on the desk while his back was facing the policemen; he got down on his knees and placed his hands behind his head as the police detained him.

September 6, 2011 10:14am

"All rise. The Honorable Judge Meahue presiding. The state of Illinois vs. Blakerian Miller. Court is now back in session." The Bailiff announced as the judge entered.

"Your honor, my client would like to take the stand." The defense spoke.

"Any objections from the State?" Judge Meahue asked.

"No objections." The State responded.

Blake rose from his seat and took the stand. He was sworn in to tell the truth by the Bailiff. Blake looked out in the audience and he saw people from Olivia's job, he saw KIT, Olivia's family members and some of his family members.

The State Attorney request to question him first. This is a tactic heavy hitter Lawyers would use. They will asked the questions they're sure the Defense would ask, but in a harsh way. They will ask uncomfortable questions to take the person off their base, so by the time the Defense starts their defense the witness is not in a calm mind and may trip over answers.

"Mr. Miller, was Dennis Hope, the person you shot and killed, having an affair with your wife?" The state asked.

"Through investigations, yes, I did find out they were intimate." Blake replied in a calm voice.

"Were you upset and angry after you found out about the affair?"

"Yes I was."

"Upset and angry, you went over to Mr. Hope with the intension to do physical harm to him. Isn't that correct Mr. Miller."

"Objection your honor." The Defense attorney shouted.

"Please withdraw or reword your question." The Judge request.

"What was your intention of going to Dr. Hope office on the 23rd day of July 2010 approximately at 2pm? It was reported you sat in the lobby for an hour. We're you there with malicious intensions?"

"No, that was not my intension; I went over to converse, man to man."

"Isn't true you were having an affair on your wife and she found out after hiring a Private-I? While you're at it, can you explain to the court who Audrey is?"

Blake sat back in his chair; he clutched his hands together and looked out into the audience at KIT. He watched her drop her head, she knew he was about to tell it all. His attorneys had no clue what he was about to say.

Blake chuckled as he began to stare at the State Attorney with an uncomfortable look. "This is everything you need to know about this case. After I present this information, I will answer no more questions nor will I make anymore statements... About 2 years ago my wife was working for this large Law firm. She was making good money; she enjoyed her job and the people she worked amongst. There were times I suspected she enjoyed her job too much. I suspect her having an affair with someone at work but I was never able to place my finger on it. I watched her behavior change at home and with me. I prayed and wished for better days with my wife, so we could have a happy life. I went to her with an entreat to reframe from any activities she was having outside of the household. I promised her we would work on having a baby. That was something she had been asking me for, but I didn't feel like we were ready for a child. My wife did a total turn around with her life at work and home. She no longer worked so many hours, we started doing things together and we would talk for hours about any and everything."

The entire court room was quiet everyone was tuned into him explaining and telling his side of the story.

"We found a fertility clinic that would accommodate our needs and our issues. We then got pregnant and life was great."

Neither the State Attorney nor the Defense Attorney knew anything about the pregnancy. So both counsels were in awe.

"We had her baby shower at seven months; the Dr. told us there was a great chance the baby would come early, so we wanted to be prepared. Her job decided to do a shower at work for her. That particular day Mr. Dennis Hope, one of her clients and her ex lover was at the shower. The entire week my wife had been complaining about the stairs at work. She explained they were doing a fitness week in the building and they shut off the elevators during lunch time so she would have to take the stairs. She was taking the stairway down to the car with some bags in her hand. I learned she was met in the stairway by Dr. Dennis Hope. I learned the conversation grew intense; he grabbed her by the arm, she yanked away from him and rolled down a couple flights of stairs. He never tried to help her; he just turned away and left down there. She was found unconscious a few broken bones and lying in a puddle of blood. She was rushed to the hospital, but... but... It was too late, she survived, but the baby, the baby, oh the baby... didn't make it."

The entire courtroom was in chills. You could see women wiping their tears. The State Attorney even turned her head as she walked back towards her table. She didn't want to show signs of weakness, but this story touched home in so many places.

Blake continued. "For months Olivia wouldn't really speak about anything or take a look at herself in the mirror. She would just sit up and look out the window. She questioned God and asked why her. All that work we did to repair our relationship was snatched from under us that day she went tumbling down the stairs. Her job gave her a pension, referred us to a quote on quote, All-Purpose-Doctor for our recovery. They told us we would not have to pay anything out of pocket, all the vis meds and counseling could be done by this Doctor and they will cover all the fees for a year. The Doctor they assigned us was Dr. Dennis Hope."

You could hear the distraught in the court room. You could hear people talking amongst themselves. "Order in the court, order in the court." The judge repeated as he pounded his gabble.

Once again Blake continued. "I found out through investigation, Dr. Hope was in a settlement and retained my wife company as his lawyers. They used the bartering system. He provides service for us for year, and they took on his case as his lawyer. That's the nature of Corporate America for you."

Once again the court began in an uproar. The Judge and Bailiff had to get the people settled before Blake was able to finish.

He proceeded. "My wife at some point thought I was having an affair and hired a Private-I. I ran into her one night snooping around my condo and following me. I approached her and asked her why was she following me? She explained to me who she was and what she was doing. She told me after a few weeks of investigating; she realized I was not having an affair. My wife had this condition if she went too many days without taking her meds, she would swear her name was Audrey. After speaking to her family, I found out Audrey was her imaginary friend when she was a kid. Audrey had a very fun side to her that I enjoyed. At times I would be kind of happy my wife didn't take her meds that meant more of Audrey. I began to fall in love with my wife Altered Ego." Blake began to raise his voice as his emotions began to rise. "Am I wrong for wanting to have fun times with my wife? Yea, I may have let her skip a couple days from taking her meds a couple times. Who are you to judge, she was being well taken care of and was in good hands. Then to realize I was spilling my beans to a guy that was fucking fucking my wife. The same guy that is responsible for taking away my child, the same guy that's responsible for my wife taking the 9mm out of the lockbox and blowing her fucking brains out once the PI told her all the stuff she discovered. So really... Am I being tried for fucking up the guy that fucked over me, fucked my wife and fucking killed my child. You know what. Fuck this. Yall finish, or yall done? I ain't got no more talking."

Blake got up from his seat and started to walk toward the door, the court was in a rage, Blake got attacked by the officers and wrestled to the ground. His family got involved and it all became a big mess in the court.

Blake end up spending the night in jail for contempt of court, really, I think they were just holding him to give him time to calm down. He eventually was release of all charges. His wife Law firm cut a deal with the state and he walked away with only the pains of the world. No one ever really heard from of saw Blake after that... And that was my last case...

THE END

This next story is a series I would like to do base on doing the wrong thing for the right reason! I am experimenting on writing to gravitate outside of my culture.

"Here we go again, same ole shit we've been going through for months." Gil said as he fixed the latched the last button on his shirt. Gilbert stood five foot eight inches from the bottom of his feet to the low-cut waves that he consistently brushed on the top of his head. An average build guy with a mediocre frame. He was a Hispanic and ready to settle in life with a wife and kids.

"You keep lingering on the things over and over again. That is how we got to where we are now. Could you get out of your feelings? We have a mission we are trying to accomplish. You know I can't be all stressed out, so please don't start with me this morning." Mena expressed as she flopped across the bed. They had decided it was time they tried for a baby. Mena, in her early thirties, was pregnant once. Her baby was still born from a previous relationship prior years before meeting Gil. Since then she has been on a health kick and made sure she maintained her five-foot two athlete figure. For years she put in numerous hours in the gym and was in no hurry to put her Hispanic body back in baby fat.

"Old things huh?" Gil said as he uneven his tie over his neck preparing to tie it.

She loved this man by all means. A lot of times in the relationship she did the wrong thing for all the right reasons. "Yes! Old things." Mena responded as she looked in his direction waiting to make eye contact.

He stares out the window with a mind full of thoughts that neglects him for loving the love of his life and his future wife. He watched cars pass by, he watched the mailman distribute mail and he also watched a house wife on his block walk her dog. "I'm not sure about all this anymore Mena."

Mena rose from the bed, "Not sure of what? The pregnancy, the marriage of you talking about us in general." She waited for his response. He just continued staring out the window while fixing his tie."

"You have me going to these doctors, questioning my manhood. They got me jacking off in a cup. Who knows who they gave my sperm to; they could be using my sperm and creating lab babies for all I know." Still he refuses to make eye contact her. "I'm tired of the arguing, the nightly fights, the questioning of are you or am I.

"So what are you saying Gil?" She asked with all of her attention on him.

"Yes Mena, I can't keep doing this with you. You deserve so much more. I know you want a baby, I keep stressing you about the past and it has not been a healthy environment the past few months." He stated as he finally turned to her. She was in shock; she knew the sacrifices made, things she has done to get pregnant so they could have the family he has always wanted with her. Tears rolled down her cheeks but no words were released from her mouth. "Mena I have an apartment on the other side of town. When I make it in from work today, I will pack up my stuff."

Mena head dropped to the pillow filled with her falling tears. Her emotions left her motionless as she watched him turn to the door. Tears, anger, hurt all blurred her vision as he exited the house and she watched the door shut behind him.

Mena pulled herself together and headed out for work. Every twenty minutes she was in the restroom throwing up. Nerves were shot, she couldn't keep anything on her stomach and she was having dizzy spells. She didn't want to go home, there were too many memories that would have only made her feel worse. One of her Co-Workers saw her behavior and reported to the department manager.

Within minutes she was addressed by her department heads. "Mena, girl is you ok? You look sickling." Her manager stated as she watched Mena pull her head from the desk.

"Oh, I'm ok. I think I may have eaten something that didn't agree with me. It's ok, I feel a lot better now." Mena explained as she turned looking for the waste catcher.

"No I don't think you are ok, do we need to call an Ambulance? You look like you are really sick; we can't have you in the office like this. You may defile others." Her manager spoke as she reached down to assist Mena out of her chair.

"No, really. I am feeling a lot better. I think I got it all out." Mena said as she rose from the chair.

"Well, we're not going to take that chance..." Before the manager could finish her sentence, Mena turned, planted her hands on her desk and began to throw up all over her keyboard and mouse.

The manager did a side step making sure none of the barf got on her. She unattached her hand from under Mena armpit so she could distance herself. She wasn't sure if she was going to throw up again, but she was sure she didn't want any of it getting on her.

As she released herself from Mena, she watched Mena body go limp. Mena's head bounced off the side of the chair, the back of her head hit the corner of the desk and forced her to face plank on the floor. The manager leaned over to see if she was ok. She saw all the vomit and immediately started vomiting on Mena back while she was knocked out. The manager rushed back to her desk and called the paramedics.

By the time the paramedics arrived, the word had spread through the office. There were a lot of people standing around trying to see what happened and asking plenty of questions. The paramedics reached the desk and saw the mess created. "What the fffffff…" He caught himself as he re-evaluated his words. "What happened here? Why is there vomit on her back?"

"Maybe she turned into the Exorcist and threw up on her back." A smart remark came from the crowd. Everyone heads tuned to see who made the comment. Mena coughs and turns to her side. Everyone began to scatter trying to make sure she didn't vomit on them. Slowly the scenery cleared as the medics got her and in the back of the Ambulance without any other episodes. They got her checked in the hospital, stabilized and drugged up so she could rest. Just before she passed out she sent a text. *"Baby, please come see me now, it's urgent!"* She passed out; her phone hit the floor and shattered.

"Man you sure she is not home?" Manny asked as they sat in th
U-Haul in the front of the yard

"Yes I'm sure." Gil replied as he looked around the truck for his keys to the house. Manny was Gil day one. He wasn't around that much since Gil got with Mena. He knew Gil was trying to settle in, have a wife and family. But anytime Gil needed a sure friend, he knew Manny would come through every time.

They make their way up to the third floor, they begin to walk towards the apartment and from afar they see a guy knocking at the door. Manny tapped Gil on the chest and whispered, "Bro, is that your apartment ole dude at?

They started walking a little slower just to be able to get a better glance. "Yea bro, that's my shit he's knocking on." Gil replied as he begar to pick up the pace.

"Well, you are moving your shit out. It's really not your shit anymore. Ya know." Gil ignored Manny as he picked up his pace trying t approach the stranger at the door.

The closer they got; the more Gil recognized the guy. "Hey dude, what the fuck you doing at my door?" Gil yelled from a far. A few more steps and they were face to face. "You gotta lotta nerves homeboy."

"Fuck you mean, your bitch called me." Rage replied. Rage was the ex-boyfriend of Mena. He is the one that was fathering the stillbirth of Mena.

"Bitch? Who you calling a bitch?" Gil asked. But, before he could reply Manny had already taken a swing that connected to Rage jaw.

Rage stumbled and Gil caught him on the chin as he was falling... Kick, kick, kick. Punch, punch, punch. You can create your own image of how the fight went. Two guys on one, this was no movie scene. When he hit the floor, his opportunity to win was no more.

"My name is Gilbert Astrong, my fiancé La'Mena Mendez has been admitted to the hospital. I went by her job, they said she got sick and was transported to this hospital. So, can someone please tell me what the fuck is going on before I go John Q in this bitch."

Security heard the tone in his voice and approached him. Gil was still on an adrenaline rush from the fight and going up to Mena's job with aggression. "Sir, you will have to calm down or we will have to detain you.

Gil looked around and saw he was outnumbered, he knew if he didn't calm down he would be detained. Gil took a deep breath as he stated, "I just want to see my fiancé. Can someone please point me in the direction to her? Please and thank you." He said as he clapped his hands together while taking a slight bow.

He was pointed in the direction of the service desk, he provided the needed information and they got him on his way to see her. As he walked through the hall to her room, he arranged in his head how the conversation would go with her. He was deeply disappointed in what he pulled out of the mailbox, he was hurt by seeing the guy at his door on top of the fact he'd already made up his mind that he could no longer be with Mena.

He enters the room, "Hey honey." Mena expressed in a woosey tone. He could tell they'd put her on meds. "Guess what honey. Guess what they told me?" He looked over to her and felt his anger rising.

Before she could tell him what she learned, he interrupted her. "The fuck was your ex doing at our door?" Mena began to sit up as she was confused. "You don't waste any time huh?"

Confused look on Mena face as she asked. "Honey what are you talking about?"

"That fuck boy Rage was at the apartment when I went back there? You thought I was at work so you just called him over huh?" He states with confidence in his voice.

"Baby, look around. I'm in the flipping hospital. How was I supposed to be at the apartment fucking a guy and in her with IV's in my arms? Do you even care why I'm in here? You haven't even asked me how I am doing." She said as she waved her hand signaling him to look around.

He dropped his head; his emotions were getting the best of him. Even though he and her were not on the best of terms, he still loved her deep down inside. "Are you ok? What happened that you're in here?" He forced out trying to hide his pain.

"I was throwing up at work. I got weak, hit my head on the desk and passed out on the floor." She replied.

"Why didn't you call me? Why did no one from your job call me and let me know?" He asked out of concern.

"I sent you a text just before I passed out. I told you to come see me, it was 911." She looked down and saw her phone lying on the floor disassembled.

"You lying. I didn't get a text from you. This just another one of these lil games you playing. He began to revert to the anger that brought him to the hospital.

She began to look confused again as she asked, "Soooo, if you didn't get my text then why are you... Or how did you know I was in the hospital?"

"After I got into it with Rage, I went by your job after I noticed you weren't in the house. They told me you were here." He said as he folded his arms getting ready to drill her with questions.

"I'm pregnant, I'm fucking pregnant." She said as laid back on the bed. "You running around causing all these problems and we are pregnant." He sat down in the chair and listened to her voice fade in and out as she continued with tears in her eyes and a tremble in her voice. "All the tests, all the procedures, running back and forth to the doctors. All of that has paid off babe. We finally did it. We Can now have that family we always wanted. Let's put our differences aside." She looked over to him. "Honey aren't you excited?"

He stood up from his seat. He reached in his back pocket and pulled out a letter. He walked over to the bed and dropped the letter in her lap. "This came in the mail today." He turned and walked away. He didn't want to look back at her. The hurt of knowing one knows is like Captain Ahab dying twice and can really be a dick. He could hear her cry out to him as he walked down the hall, but his pride, his hurt and his conscience would not allow him to turn back.

"Mom, I'm going to dry my hair and I will be right in there?" Millie spoke as she was getting out of the shower. Millie is Mena's daughter and she promised to tell her about her dad before she turned Fifteen.

"Ok sweetie." Mena responded with anxiety in voice. She knew this story would force her to relive a time capsule in her life that she tried to abandon.

Millie meets her mom at the table. "Mom are you sure you want to do this? You look so nervous." Millie stated as she took her seat across from her mom.

"This is long overdue my child; and there is no one else deserves this truth more than you." Mena expressed as she placed a slight grin on her face.

"Ok, lay it all on me." Millie requested.

"I'm going to just get right to it." Mena said as she placed one hand inside of her other and planted them on the table.

Millie took a deep breath. "Take your time mom."

Mom, fifteen years later and that phrase still doesn't get old to her. "Back in 2004 a few months before you were born, I had a life changing incident with the man that should have been your father."

"Should have been?" Millie asked.

"Yes, should have been." Mena responded. "There was this guy by the name of Rage. He was a handsome man. I met him when I was really young and eager for excitement. We ended up getting pregnant. We went out and bought all the baby stuff. Set Up a room for the baby and made a play date to get married after the baby was born." Mena got silent; it was as if she put herself on pause.

"Mom, are you ok?" Millie asked as she reached her hands out to cover her mom's hands.

""Yes daughter, I'm fine." She explained as she unmuted herself.

"Mom, really we can do this another time." Millie requested.

"No, the time is now." Her mom insisted. "The baby was born early and it wasn't moving." Tears began to roll down Mena cheeks. "I felt that I let him down. I had one job, that was to carry his child. I didn't have to work, cook or clean. My job was to carry his child. I couldn't do that." She said as she burst into tears and placed her hands over her face.

Millie unseated herself and walked around the table to her mom. "Mom. Please, you don't have to do this." She said as she wrapped her arms around her mom.

Mena removed her hands from her face and continued. Her story. "After I loss the baby he changed. He was not the same person. I know he loved me but I couldn't see the love. I never stopped loving that man. I moved on with my life, but I continued to love him."

"What happened to him? Where did he go?" Millie asked.

"Let me finish sweetie." Mena said. "Rage would come around from time to time. He never really left out of my life. He stayed his distance when needed, but he was always there. But then I met Gil. Gil showed me life. He showed me how to survive with the tools I have. He taught me to never be afraid of leaning on someone or something, but to make sure you are prepared if and when it falls."

"Is Gil my dad?" Millie asked.

Mena opened the floodgates and started to cry again. "Gil, oh Gil." She repeated a couple times as she was being caressed by her daughter.

"I'm not sure I want to know about my father. This is too much and too painful for you mom."

"No, no honey. I really need to do this for you, and for me as well. I promise, I will be strong and try and not break down." Mena gave a smile as she waited for assurance from her daughter.

"You promise mom?"

"I promise honey." She said as she embraced her embracing. So, Gil and I decided we wanted to have a baby. There were a lot of complications. We tried for months. So we decided to get ourselves tested. My results came back a lot quicker; everything checked out well with me. It took over 2 weeks for us to get Gil results. One night we were out on the town we ran into Rage. He was already a little tipsy. He made the comment, 'There goes the baby momma of my dead child'. It put Gil in an awkward mood. Words were exchanged and temperatures were in flames as we all parted ways. About a week later I got a call from the fertility lab. They told Gil was the reason we weren't getting pregnant. They said he has a very slim chance of ever getting anyone pregnant."

It was like she put herself on mute again. "Mom, mom. Mom, mom." Millie repeated.

"Yes dear, sorry. I couldn't find the words I needed." Mena continued. "Gil was already on an edge, he felt less than a man being tha we were having issues getting pregnant. Soooo." She hung on to so that for about a second. "One day I reached out to Rage while I was on my high ovulating days and we hooked up several times.

Millie snatched away from her mom. "So you're the reason my father left me?"

Mena had to stay strong; she knew this wasn't going to be an easy task.

"Honey listen." Mena pleaded.

"All these years I'm thinking my father was a sleaze and a dirt bag for leaving his daughter. And all the while you got pregnant from another guy and were going to pin the baby on him?" Millie said in a tone of discuss.

"Baby, it's not that simple. I loved both men. I wouldn't trade the blessing I got from all of this. You are my sunshine; you gave me reasons to breathe the days I didn't have a breath."

"Wow mom. I would have never thought in a million years you would stoop so low." Millie said.

"You will not sit here and disrespect me; I did what I had to do to get you here. I have spent the past fifteen years harboring these emotions. Now sit yo lil narrow ass down so I can finish my story." Mena said as she pointed at the seat.

Mena walked over and reseated herself across from her mom. "So, how did Gil find out?

"Gil and I were going through a breakup just before I found out I was pregnant."

"I can imagine that." Millie said under her voice.

Mena gave her the mean eye just before she finished her story. "Gil left for work, he came back to the house and Rage was standing outside the door."

"Whooooaaaa." Millie expressed. "Why was he there?"

"I got sick at work that day and was rushed to the hospital. I thought I was sending Gil a text, but it was a text to Rage. The text said come see me it's an Emergency." Mena paused.

"Take your time mom. It's going to be ok." Millie stated.

"They had a confrontation; Rage was never seen or heard from since. Gil came to the hospital with papers in his back pocket. I told him I was pregnant, he pulled out the papers mailed from the fertility clinic stating that he has less than a ten percent chance of ever getting anyone pregnant."

"Damn mom, that's really fucked up." Mena expressed.

"You watch your mouth." Millie yelled. "Honey, I have made some horrible decisions in my life. But I can promise you, what I was trying to do with Gil was genuine and from my heart. That was just a case of me doing the Wrong Thing For The Right Reason!"

The next two writings titled (Jilter and Last One) are poetic stories. They coincide (one with the other) and are designed to poetically paint a picture through the rhymes.

Jilter

Their convention promised pertinent stability and offered a lifetime of contingency,

Their families reverenced their compassion for love and found comfort in their intimacy.

Her innocence were pure and she attain no knowledge and a man she had never known,

The first time they laid face-to-face clothe-less their true feelings were sparingly shown.

She loved him for the things she liked within his soul that soothed her tensional yearn,

He liked the things that made him love her deferentially as it kerosene his lantern to burn.

Three years of courtship maximized their capacity for reliance down the promising path,

God couldn't have created man without the woes and she was his womb less the wrath.

Complacent was his satisfaction and her affirmation that this correlation was heaven sent,

Set in ways and confined to the related agreement, until one episode not a rule was bent.

Started out with a girls night out while the guys slumbered in PJ's with board games,

She got a taste of more than just nightlife when loomed by a fellow requesting names.

His proposal statements were unblemished to ears of bodies that defied a new adventure,

Knowing right from wrong, but it's not wrong if never caught are beliefs of the immature.

Stars spangled while she mangled the trust earned with a known stranger to elevate her,

Hearts tangled as curiosity angled her attention to deter from that one at home she call sir.

From thus night forward she reached out to others that placed a strain on her initial plan,

His love remains the same being he's vowing to death do them part and he was her man.

No fool ever he claimed to be for he saw the change of how things use to be but he loved,

Encouraged by the outcome and not acceptant to the outlook the concrete he bottled and gloved.

One hundred eighty days of agony he watched her drift to and fro in the double life,

She couldn't control her dependence and began slithering the obligations of a future wife.

Hind feet no doubt were in her possession but the blind side she chose with her eyes wide,

She knew his precedent forced him to reside aside from her wrong to keep him by her side.

The date was set; the flowers were picked, invitations were sent, families bonded for the unification,

The pastor counseled, the deacons ordained, the congregation approved the wedding preparation.

Not once did he ever persist to revisit the scenes of anti-trust for he learn that wouldn't help,

A straight face he retained approaching the wedding date, but the Lord knows the feelings felt.

Wedding scheduled 2008, everyone was on time, Chaplin, ring barrier, flower girl, even the black folk weren't late.

His and her mother comforted her congratulating her on her turn of character that allowed her to get to this date.

"Shit still funny to me cause I didn't even tell me best man or family members about how it was going down.

I prayed the week before after I asked the guy to make the announcement that presented the news dress as a clown."

"After I wasn't found an hour after the ceremony started, the guy made his way down the aisle asking for the wife to-be.

When she came out he presents her the personal journal she kept and told her she can now be free."

Astounded she was but she knew what the journal entailed as the tears fell from her face to the floor.

"Cry not now" the clown announced as he pulled out pieces of papers as she anguish to see what more.

"The bitch wrote about how she slept with my cousin the first girl's night out and how it was an itch that needed to be scratch.

When I confronted my cousin she covered the story up and claimed she passed out from the alcohol and woke up in a cane patch."

Many other adventures I read about with episodes she had that ranged from women, men, and even an under aged girls.

As the clown got back in the car I cried jilted tears of revenge on my wedding day for the person I put before my world.

Last One
(Jilted)

Last One
(Jilted)

At junctures throughout her life she would visually visualized from
beginning to end the script to become the perfect wife.
She often had dreams of her groom that presented himself hidden
behind the woes and scars she carried that cut like a knife.

Vividly she could describe her virtual prize with ignited closed eyes that
kept her thoughts mesmerized while filling her loneliest space.
For days she would be in replay mode wishing for that someone to hold
but as colorful as dreams were she could never see his face.

In a particular time, while her mind was in rewind, vulnerable, she was
verbally apprehended by a guy interested in her interest to learn.
Good wishes giving while her ivory glisten the instant while conversing
marinated the patients, she could see the night was about to take a turn.

Talking lead to walking, drinking stopped them from thinking, thinking
about the things that were parting them to break their shell.
Spare you I shall of that night and its detail, I'm sure we're all familiar of
what happens between male and female; let's just say it finished well.

It was two worlds combined to take on the world; everyday was like a
new episode of boy meets girl, the love stretched like a country mile.
She felt like she was the reason Hall and Oak wrote that song about Sarah
being each day he gave her a transparent reason to smile.

His "Her", most definitely she was, and without any hesitation she knew
where she stood and acknowledged her feet were on solid grounds.
Her "Him" he stood proud speaking with his chest any opportunity he
was given to express kind gestures whether or not if she was around.

Written thoughts of love carried her through the days of grudge knowing
on this side the grass really is green.

Plaster filled captured moments assured him their journey was destine and he was delighted to be a part of the team.

Adventurous they were at times, role playing, public sexing escapades, living the life and setting the sky as the limits.
Fearful to be without fear was the motive, let all emotions run a rant and give nothing the opportunity to get you timid.

The spring of 2012, deep within the Flora's the flowers begin to dwell, he had a special day coming up and she wanted it to be memorable.
She promised him a planned night, somewhere near the moon lite, where the ocean breeze was right, pledging it will be unforgettable.

Never did he question detail of what was entailed, as long as it involved she, he was insanely satisfied just to breathe the same air as her.
She couldn't have given in to a better guy, and they say sex on the 1st date relation don't last, that's a lie, even when drunken his love never slur.

Once the Sun settled their day and all the grown folk came out to play, she made sure he would be gratified in the upmost way.
An evening like no other, things were about to go down that he wouldn't tell his mother, on this night "nothing gold would stay."

They went out to a swingers club… Yes that's right, a swingers club, a few drinks and minutes to mingle to get a feel of the spot.
They integrated with a couple of their interest that had been subliminally discussed but never really mentioned, it was a female couple, and they were HOTT!

As much as she loved the monogamy, she understood a man still has fantasies, and this was his night to fulfill a passion.
She vowed to not participate; she was raggin and didn't want anyone to touch her plate, from the outside she decides to watch the action.

The two girls were doing things she's never seen, mental note she were taking of each scene, she knew this was his life win.
She couldn't help but to feel bad inside, several times she almost cried, it was hard for her to stomach the internal sin.

Later that night they made it back to their room, too drunken to give a real proposal to be her groom, he pulled out a ring and plunged down on one knee.

He told her he's the one that came to her at night, and his face was hidden by the light, and just before he passed out he asked, "Will you marry me?"

It's Ironic she never told him about the dream; before she could answer she was staring at her sleeping King, Queen for the moment she was in her mind.

Tears slicing through her makeup to the pillow, she cried more that night than a pregnant widowed, but the darkest nights still have morning shine.

He awoke that morning hung-over to a dry reality, in an all-white room looking like he has just stepped out of heaven, but there was a letter left on the bed.

She was nowhere in sight, it's like she vanished in the night, but she left all the details in the letter and this is what it said:

"You have been more than too good to me; there were times through my glass I though you could see, though you are my virtual reality we could never be.

The girls last night were staged, both of them have Aids, thus is why no protection or participation from me, and I quote, "You Can Now Be Free"!

In 2009 a beautiful young lady hung herself in her prime, because she saw life and just wanted to have a good time, but all she worked for is wilted.

That young lady was dear to my heart, so I sought revenge to get back the parts that were left at the altar of the Last One you Jilter."

The next era of art is my foundation of my gift. This is what comes natural to me, poetry. There are a variety of poems; my wife challenged me to write against lyrics, Pass the pen topic to other writers, picture poetry and more...

An Open Plea

Your soul is ready to take me places my
heart won't allow me to go;
my body's your subject matter completing
an indirect sin each time I say no.

I'm just writing thoughts I'm thinking
randomly while I'm in this moment of time,
Please don't critique the errors and
decipher what you can use between the line.

How often do we ask for the heart and
not even sure if we're ready for that great show,
How many times have we've come in
contact with a heart and just saw it as a Love's Logo.

Pay me no mind I'm just wasting time tryna
think of things that rhyme so I can fill the next line,
If you caught Dex in his prime I know you memba the
times I spoon fed souls while swinging vine to vine.

That lifestyles been retaught Imma man of many flaws a
few run in with the laws but he forgave me for what I saw.
Those were just current events once again this is my chance
to vent I won't give it up even for lent but do I miss it... Hell2Da Naw.

Well this was my open plea giving me a chance to speak
free if you didn't know all of the above is a snippet about me.
Those are just some of my random thought in conjunction
with some struggles I've fought imma skip pt2 and go str8 to pt3.

Game Card

A game of spades consists of 52 cards, 13 of each suite.

A new deck contains 54 playing cards and a few other flukes.

Two jokers are at times questioned should they be a part of the game.

When you implement them there are new rules and set different terrains.

A spade is a black heart turned upside down with a support.

Pause; Blackened hearts represents being burned, like with a torch.

Hands are held close and never displayed to let one see your play.

At what point we show our hearts risking it all for that one that we say.

We care dearly and wouldn't mind sharing our diamonds we posses.

And would Club any one in a club that brings upon any disrespect.

Cards on the table, blacken hearts or traditional red, you call the shot.

Though it may be hard, it's better doing than say you did and not.

Pen Passing (LOVE)

I don't curse but in this verse... Hole-up my origin is greater than anything that's been rehearsed.

I could start by saying I leave your P in a hearse, but that contradicts line one plus I'm for hers.

I use to write in pencil, til realizing sealing my pen was only a filter and it was no longer necessary.
Now I touch my pen, til spilling my ink, let that lead fly shooting up the club, pull it out & slang it eva-be-ware.

If you know me, you know I'm big on words, profanity is needed not for description, nor do I feel love really do exist.
But the acronym for LOVE, I stand firm to my beliefs of, my done and not said; to the known this is more than a myth.

Leaving
Ovaries
Voluptuous
Every time... ... ...
Penetrates and extracts your inner halls creates friction preceded to swe
your walls; Hey that rhyme.

Licking
Over
Vaginal
Entrance... ... ...
Before entering the misfit salivating... no I use my spit to moisturize before pulverizing is how I take my stance.

Legs
Open
Very
Easily... ... ...

Subjecting and erecting the circumstance is now a situation resulting with pre-ejaculating thoughts of pleasing.

Other acronyms like: Lusting One Vajayjay Every day, Letting Others Vigorously Eat, Long Oversizes Vaccinates Eruptions...
And ooh ooh: Libra Obsessively Vanishing Erector, Left Opulent & Vacant Exceedingly, are the writers' acr for readers' seductions.

All holes are options when performing an autopsy, one must Perspex from various angles.
Yea yea I know, the first two opening are a given, thumbs up to the women letting play within the anal.

I could have used terms such as dick, pussy, ass, suck and fuck.
Creativity in passing the pen to the follow up, hope you possess a set of skills... Good luck!

Wife:

There's a candle that's burning in my heart tonight. And the flame is full of my desire. And I can't help but desire you in my bed tonight. And I'll touch you in the places no one's been before and I'll kiss you in the place men sometimes ignore and I'll take you to a level you never been before

And though you won't understand it you'll cry and ask for more
Jon B. "Pretty Girl"

Now write me your version...challenge.

Me:

Candles lit by flames I ignited that night in our bed.
The desire to get you higher, I'm metaphorically in your head.

The wonders of your touch salivate un-wiped drools left by fools that couldn't appreciate;
You or your passion they were too busy acting, no focus on lasting to penetrate that save the date.

Is it for me that you bliss, or the most affectionate simile of a kiss?
Nah, I cashed in all my hope that day God granted you to me as a wish.

Ignorance is not rooted by the word ignore, nor do I when your concern are asking for more.
Jon B writers couldn't out write me even if my hands were tied behind the writer's block door.

Tell that white guy you met the right guy and his words are of the Powerless Ranger.
So the next time challenged rhyme for rhyme, know that I'm the crime, and beware of my lyrical anger.

Too Easy

Wife:

 you fire bae I swear. You win

I'm cheesin

Me:
You should.
Thanks for the force write.

I smiled when I got the challenged. Pulled over and executed.

Kis-Her-Toe

Every year she want me to kiss her under that stupid branch folk call a mistletoe;
I keep the eggnog coming assuring my kisses touch both lips, under her camel-toe

Feeding Mrs. Claus, one Tequila, two tequilas, three then I pick her up from the flo;
Every since we updated our status, I have vowed to be the protector and also her whore-hoe-ho.

Told me when her status change from sing-gul, her gul loses her vocals and forget to sing;
That lullaby she was chirping the last time made me want to go out and buy her another ring.

We go Kong forever Kingless but beasting if you know what I mean;
To the uneducated she has been granted all rights to this linga that dings

Mr. Claus(me) permits usage of the FedEx method when it's time for us to be a lil savage;
She can get it three day priority, 2nd day guarantee, or even the overnight package.

Her ragga ragga ragga studies my movement and I match her choreography;
My jagga jagga jagga moves to her studies and reacts to her snatch on X-Mas eve.

Walnuts explain our finale, but, chestnuts what's use as foreplay.
If there's nuts on the chin, whelp, you know what they say... Happy Holiday!

BEAUTIFUK

Bending you over and pleasuring your asset
Engages an erection for your complexion;
Angles positions ur pussi'n premed pushing
Utter air grasp of words explain our sexxion.
Toe tingle touching, saliva slanging sucking
Intensifies the freak that hides what we say;
Fuck this pussi, suck this dick yea all of that
Unleashed graphically in our moment of slay.
K replaced by L, allowing this Beautifuk day!

Arithmetic

Math was my strength and until current, I use it to advance your weakness.
Fractions woe'd to you being you never wanted a part, all is your meekness.

Division of your unparalleled legs formulates a greater than sign while I taste your Pi.
Multiplying the velocity as I enter and re-enter your Circumference is never a question of why.

The numerous times we put our Variables together creates an Algebraic expression.
Parenthesis models your bowlegs as I FOIL First Out In Lasting through our session.

Subtraction of the latex every since you sent that late text speaking the Statistic all point in the Right Angle.
Trig is a mixture of Geometry, Physics a sprinkle of Calculus defining our Chemistry while working on an addition when we tangle.

The equation may vary do to the sum and other probabilities, but, just know.
Each word problem we may have is a Finite of what our heart will really show.

All Math ends with an Equal as we encounter love.
Please solve what's being presented in the lines above!

The last sections are writings of stories I have yet to finish. I love, love, love both of these writings, but I have struggled to find the time to finish them. Hopefully sometime soon I will.

Rope, Tree, Hang

Tube speaks, "You think this is about race huh? That's why you keep calling the police Crackas. Tube, a middle age black male trying to was a straight and narrow to keep his family from feuds.

Curb responded, "Cause, dats wat dey are... Crackas. It don't matter wat dey skin color. If dey get up errr morn, put on dem clown blu uniforms, den dats wat dey are... CRACKAS!"

"Curb, mofo you're the Protestant of the White Anglos Saxons. You grew up privileged. Your parents put you in a private so you could ge a good education. You were too lazy to do the work so you dropped out of Middle School, ran away and you been in the hood every since." Tube expressed with anger in his tone.

"Man, I aint wanna be round dem square ass preppy kids." Curb said as he pulled out his lighter to fire up his Black.

"First off!" Tube stated as he paused while holding up his finger symbolizing there is more to come. "I ain't wanna be, is improper grammar. Had you stayed in any school you would have learn that. Second of all..." He paused again as he held up two fingers. "Those same preppy ass kids are becoming Governors, Senates and Judges that are setting the same laws that keep putting your hood mentally in jail."

"Yea whateva man." Curb said as he lit his Black. He remembere kids in class talking about one day being the President, having a lot of power and being able to help run the Country. While being in the hood, everyone just wants to be rich to get out. "So, what you saying Tube?" F asks after taking a drag.

"What I'm saying is look around you. It's not only blacks in the hood. There is a diverse of cultures that have their own hood. Trailer trash, Ghetto, China Town, Oye's and everywhere else. The Government doesn't care about the color of your skin, or at night how you ask to be forgiven for your sins. Your gold teeth, pants to your knees tattoo arm sleeves will get you the Minority treatment for trying to blend in."

"So through theoretically, if I comprehend what you're attempting to get me to apprehend." Curb put down his Black to entertain Tube respectfully as he continued. "If the Judicial proctors are really hunting the gatherers, and forcefully administering irregular lawful treatments. Riddle me this, why would they let me go thrice on a gun charge? With the same gun each time?"

"I'm glad you ask Curb." He was not surprised by the intelligence Curb displayed. "Back in the day, your kind, road around in big trucks, burn crosses and hung people to trees. Notice I didn't say black people; much like the myth that Abe freed the slaves, blacks wasn't the only ones apart of the lynching. As time grew people like me caught on and realizing they don't hang people anymore. They hand them the rope show them the tree and watch them hold on to the other side as they hang themselves."

Curb shifted his body weight to reposition for the remaining of Tube lecture. "Ok, and your point?"

"Did they give you probation?" Tube asked.

"Yes" Curb answered.

"What address they force you to use?" Tube quizzed.

"I used the same address I been living at in the past few years." Curb responded with a confusing look.

"So they handed you probation. That's your Rope! They make sure when they check up on you, you're in the same area in which you commit crimes. That gives you the opportunity to pick your Tree. Then they sit back, watch and ignore the ignorance as you go commit another crime to 'provide for your family' and you Hang Yourself.... ROPE... TREE... HANG"

Be Like Santa

Be Like Santa

"Blue pill or the red pill? Fuck, I can't keep this up year after year. I feel like Morpheus and need to hand this shit off to Neo." Santa expressed as he packed his bag for his long night. Santa has earned and lived up to his name for years. (S.A.N.T.A - Sexually Attractive Negro Tentatively Aroused).

Santa stood about five foot nine inches. He was an older gentleman in his mid fifties. He was fit for his age. He wasn't muscular, but you could see the trails of his youthful workouts. His body was solid but with a hint of a rehab Dad-Bod. "Honey, are you all packed up for the night out?" One of his little elves asks as she cuddled up in the bed covering her nudity.

She met Santa while he was on his Christmas Eve runs about three years ago. "This shit not getting old to you Clause?" Santa asked as he looked over to her watching her smile fade.

"We been in and out of people houses the past couple years. We have taken on more stops this year than we have in any other years." Clause has been Santa mate over the past three Christmas. The request for couples and other strange things have been at an all time high.

She hopped out the bed exposing her nude body, she meshed her clothe less body against the back of his manly skin. She wrapped her arm under his arm pits and gripped the top of his shoulders while pressing her face against his back. "Hun, just think about all the money that will collected tonight. This one night is worth it. All the new people you will meet, all the gifts and the experiences. Oh the experiences." She said as she played scenes from the previous year. Clause stood about five foot two inches, dirty blonde naturally curly hair and she could pass as a light skinned black girl or a well tanned white chick. She was a former stripper that fell off the pole and broke her leg. After she recovered she had a fear to dance in the club. She still enjoys entertaining others, so meeting Santa after responding to his 'What Does The Lonely Do at Xmas' she knew this was something she was interested in doing.

She rides the sleigh with Santa each year along with two others (Sugarplum Mary and Pepper Minstix) that fills those special request that Santa along can't or won't provide. Sugarplum Mary was a natural white chick with long stringy brunette hair. She stood five foot five inches before her Elf Heels. She looked very frail, but she weighed in as a Heavy Weight Champ when it was performance time. Pepper Minstix lived up to his name. He was sweet with stripes, but would spin it any way the customer would prefer.

"In the next few hours we need to be heading out, the sun is going down." Santa yelled across the house making sure he was heard by everyone.

"I have been waiting since last year for this moment to come." Minstix stated in an excited tone as he made his way to the room.
"Oh, I need to see the final Naughty and Nice List. I hope that one couple is on the list." Santa looked at him with a slight face of discuss. That couple almost got Santa and his elves off course from completing their rounds last year.

"Minstix, you just make sure you have the proper toys when it's your time to play. No repeats of last year. It took you months to rid that ail you had in you. One night of pleasure is not worth a life time of pain." Santa said as he exits the room.

Giggles bounced off the wall from the other side of the room. "The fuck you giggling at Mrs. Ho Ho Hoe. You want me to tell Santa about night you say you had "too much Egg-Nog"!" The giggling stopped from Clause immediately. "Oh cat got your tongue now. You had plenty of words when you let the guy dressed like Rudolf and his group of Reindeers fill all your Ho, hoe, holes." Her face drooped as she looked away in shame. "Don't close your mouth now; you should have been closing it that night." Minstix said as he turned to exit the room.

"Everyone all set, we're heading out the door in 15 minutes." Santa expressed.

"I'm ready, as usual." Minstix Chanted as he strutted towards the door with his bags.

"I made need about sixteen or seventeen minutes, y'all know I'm such a lady." Clause said as she stood in the mirror doing last minute touchups.

"Anybody seen Sugarplum?" Santa asked.

"You know she will do anything for that Sugar. She will easily give away her plum." Minstix said with laughter under his breath.

"What would you know about her plum, the only time you even see plums are when we're doing these runs?" Clause shouted from the bathroom.

"Ho, Hoe, Holessssssssss!" Minstix said to silence Clause, once again.

Sugarplum was a different from the rest of the crew. She had no limitations. There was almost nothing she would do. He limits were limitless. There were pros and cons with her. She fulfilled the exceptiona strange request that paid handsomely more than the others and she never asked for an addition for doing them. With that, she would experiment with anything.

"She left earlier when you and Clause were back there HO-HO-Hoeing. I think she heard y'all and got stimulated. She said she was goin to the bar to have a few before the night." Minstix said.

"So Minstix, you just left her leave?" Santa asked with Anger.

"That's a grown fucking lady, and you need to watch your mouth unless you planning on letting me put something in it."

Santa just raised his hands and headed towards the door. "I'm heading to the bar to see if I could find her. "Santa stated as he walked out the house.

Santa walked in the door of the bar and there was a line. The line was in an unusual spot. There was a line of guys waiting to get behind th bar. "No cutting the line sir. You gone have to wait your turn like the res of us." An anxious guy mentioned as he held his arm out to block the path of Santa.

"Oh no, I'm here looking for the white gir..." Santa sentence was cut short.

"Yes, we know we are all here in line for the white girl that's doing the lines of the white girl. Now wait your turn." Another eager guy replied.

Santa stepped out the line and took the long way to the bar. As he got closer to the other end he could see Sugarplum doing lines off the bar, but she was on the bartending side and it looked like she was stoop over. He stepped up to peep over the bar and she saw a guy bare dick plugging her anal. "This Chic" he said aloud for only him to hear. As he looked a little closer he saw there was another guy laying adjacent to the anal plugging guy, but under SugarPlum. "So she riding this guy dick and letting the other guy fuck her in the ass?" He said aloud once again for him to hear. "But I know this guy nuts have to be touching the other guys...?" He stopped his sentence in thought of the visual of what may be taking place underneath. "Plum, Plum. WTF you doing?" He shouted in a soft harsh voice.

She looked saw Santa and flinched. "Hey Santa, I was just getting fluffed and ready for our night out." She said in a voice that didn't express a concern of her doings.

"It's go time and show time." He softly yelled in a harshly. "You got a double penetration going on and we down there waiting on you. You doing lines of coke, while you got a line of dick waiting to stretch your insides. What the fuck Plum?"

She stood up and started yelling. "Off of me, everybody get the fuck off of me. Leave me along." She leaned over to Santa with the bottom part of her clothing missing. "I'm sorry Santa, how can I make this up to you? What is it that I need to do? Tell Santa Tell me?"

At that moment Santa realized he was not the favor person in the bar.... TO BE CONTINUED... ... ...